AUDREY COVINGTON BREAKS THE RULES

ALSO BY KARINA EVANS

Grow Up, Tahlia Wilkins!

AUDREY COVINGTON BREAKS THE RULES

KARINA EVANS

LITTLE, BROWN AND COMPANY
New York Boston

Interior design by Gabrielle Chang.

Little, Brown and Company
Hachette Book Group
1290 Avenue of the Americas, New York, NY 10104
Visit us at LBYR.com

First Edition: April 2023

Library of Congress Cataloging-in-Publication Data
Names: Evans, Karina, author, illustrator.
Title: Audrey Covington breaks the rules / Karina Evans.
Description: First edition. | New York : Little, Brown and Company, 2023. | Audience: Ages 8–12. | Summary: Eleven-year-old Audrey Covington and her grandmother, a former famous actress, have a night out in Hollywood where they break the rules of Audrey's strict parents.
Identifiers: LCCN 2022009101 | ISBN 9780316340427 (hardcover) | ISBN 9780316340694 (ebook)
Subjects: CYAC: Grandmothers—Fiction. | Actors and actresses—Fiction. | Rules—Fiction. | Parent and child—Fiction. | LCGFT: Fiction.
Classification: LCC PZ7.1.E8696 Au 2023 | DDC [Fic]—dc23
LC record available at https://lccn.loc.gov/2022009101

ISBNs: 978-0-316-34042-7 (hardcover), 978-0-316-34069-4 (ebook)

Printed in the United States of America

LSC-C

Printing 1, 2023

AUDREY COVINGTON BREAKS THE RULES

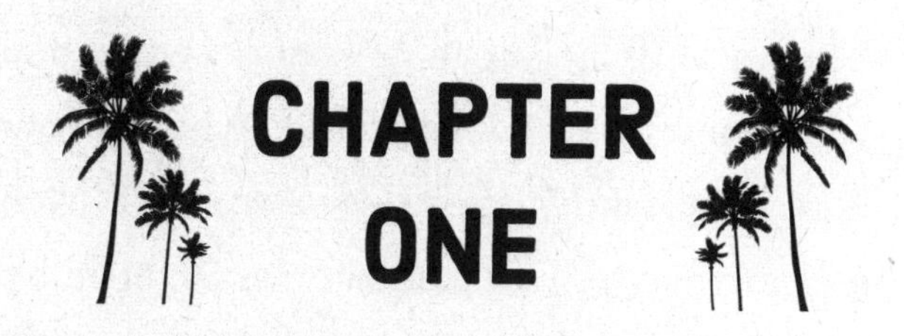

CHAPTER ONE

I THINK THIS annoying song will be stuck in my head for the rest of my life.

Two months ago, when Miss Rose first played it for our sixth-grade class, I was actually *excited* to learn it. I thought it was the perfect choice for our graduation performance since its lyrics are all about remembering good times and staying close with our friends forever—both things I plan to do, obviously.

But now, after practicing it about a million times, I think I'd be okay with never hearing it again. I've officially decided I do *not* like it. There are only so many times you can sing the same words over and over before they stick themselves to the inside of your brain. I even caught myself humming the melody as I brushed my teeth last night. At least once this graduation ceremony is over, I'll never have to hear it again.

More importantly, when this ceremony is over, I'll be an elementary school graduate. Junior high, here I come!

Squee!!

As my class starts singing the next verse, I look out into the small crowd of parents in the audience. Mom and Dad are sitting in the third row behind my best friend Sadia's parents. Well, I'm 99 percent sure that's Dad next to Mom. He's holding his phone sideways in front of his face—probably to record the performance—so I can't see his telltale bushy mustache. Mom is easier to spot. Her brown hair is in its usual neat low ponytail, and her hands are folded in her lap as she smiles up at me.

Miss Rose had our class line up alphabetically by last name, so I'm standing on stage next to Dylan

Cohen, who I'm pretty sure is singing the wrong lyrics on purpose for laughs. And it's really throwing me off! Even though I'm so done with this song, our parents are watching us, and Mom and Dad wouldn't like it if I didn't do what I was told.

If *I* purposely sang the wrong words, Mom would give me that look where she scrunches her eyebrows together, and Dad would cross his arms and sigh—like I've disappointed them. I hate the way that feels. Best to just avoid it.

However, Sadia and my other best friend, Tamzin (lucky ducks who both have last names starting with *H*), seem to think Dylan's incorrect lyrics are funny. Out of the corner of my eye, I can see them standing together, holding back giggles and trying to sing with straight faces.

I wish I were over with them. Maybe I'd also think Dylan's singing is funny if I weren't *right* next to it. Oh well. At least I'll get to spend all day with my friends tomorrow at our annual end-of-year slumber party.

Woot woot!

The slumber party is a tradition we started during

the summer after finishing third grade—the first summer my parents let me even have sleepovers. Ever since, on the first Saturday after finishing the school year, we spend the entire day over at Tamzin's house and say *sayonara!* to the previous grade. It's our ritual.

But *this* year, the sleepover is extra important because it's also the last time I'll get to hang out with my friends before we start middle school. Sadia is spending all summer at a gymnastics sleepaway camp in Arizona, and Tamzin is going to a summer youth e-sports program in San Francisco. So, basically, other than doing chores and wishing my friends were home, I have no idea what I'll be up to during the break.

I asked Mom and Dad if I could join Sadia at the gymnastics camp, but they said no, since the sport was way too dangerous because of all the possible knee and neck injuries. And I didn't even bother asking about going with Tamzin to San Francisco, because my parents don't let me play video games. They think they're bad for my brain development or whatever.

I probably should've argued a bit more when Mom and Dad said no, but to be honest, since I've never tried the activities, I'm not even sure I *like* gymnastics or e-sports, so I wasn't positive the activities were worth Mom's scrunched-eyebrow look and Dad's crossed arms and sigh.

Tomorrow's sleepover is really the only thing I'm looking forward to before starting seventh grade, so it absolutely must be awesome.

The song finally ends, and Miss Rose hustles to the podium at the side of the stage and speaks into the mic.

"That was lovely!" She puts her hand on her heart as if that weren't the millionth time she's heard us singing it. "Let's have another round of applause for these sixth-grade graduates before I call out their names and hand out the diplomas."

The small crowd of parents claps.

When the noise dies down, Miss Rose leans closer to the mic. "Parents, thank you so much for all your support over these last seven years. From kindergarten to now, it's been such a joy getting to know your children." She turns her smile back to us up on the stage. "Everyone here at Burbank Valley Elementary wishes you the very best in junior high and beyond."

I give her a big grin back. I really like Miss Rose, and it still doesn't feel real that I'm going to be leaving her and this school behind. It's kind of weird to picture myself as a seventh grader. People in junior high have always seemed so...I don't know...big and confident, I guess—like they know where they belong.

At least I'll have Sadia and Tamzin with me. And I know I belong with them. The three of us have been best friends since before kindergarten. I can't even exactly remember the first time we met—*that's* how long I've known them. And we're going to be friends forever.

I lean forward in line to try to catch their eyes and give them a smile, but neither Sadia nor Tamzin is looking my way.

"Now." Miss Rose looks down at a piece of paper on the podium and pushes her glasses higher up on her nose. "When I call your name, please come down to collect your diploma." She clears her throat. "Damien Aarons."

The parents applaud as Damien, a tall kid with spiky black hair who once got his leg stuck in one of the railings on the playground, walks over to where Miss Rose stands at the podium. She holds out her hand for Damien to shake before taking his rolled-up diploma and returning to his spot on the stage.

Then Miss Rose calls Amber Aguilar, Nadia Bell, and Timothy Bryant. They all shake her hand and collect their diplomas.

"Dylan Cohen."

Dylan steps forward, and I stand up a little taller.

This is it. I'm next.

This is my final moment as a sixth grader.

I take a deep breath.

"Audrey Covington."

A jolt of electricity runs through me as I quickly march toward Miss Rose. I have to focus on walking so that I don't trip in front of everyone. That would be a horrible way to finish out the year.

Right foot. Left foot. Right foot. Left foot.

I can feel the audience staring at me. It makes my neck go all hot and uncomfortably tingly. I wish they'd all look away.

I guess I should explain *why*. My mom's mom—my

Nana Rhea—is an old famous Hollywood star. Ever heard of the movie *Beauty in the Wind*? Yeah, she was in that. Loads of other movies too. After she won her Oscar, the front page of the Los Angeles newspaper called her "The Leading Lady of a Generation." When Nana Rhea showed me that old headline, my mouth instantly went all dry and my stomach felt all wobbly and stretched, like it'd gone through a taffy puller. I mean, I knew my Nana Rhea had been famous, but before then, I hadn't known she was *that* famous. It felt like a lot to live up to, especially since in that same article, Nana Rhea was quoted as saying that she had known acting was her calling ever since she was a child.

I've never felt a "calling" or anything like that. Unlike Sadia with gymnastics or Tamzin with e-sports, I don't have a main thing. I guess I'm not sure what my calling is yet.

Luckily, since all of Nana Rhea's movies came out a long time ago and are really only watched by adults, Sadia, Tamzin, and the other kids at school don't know or care who my grandma is. And therefore, they don't expect me to live up to her star-power reputation.

Grown-ups, though, are a whooole different story. Once they find out I'm related to Rhea Covington, they assume I'm comfortable being in the spotlight. But truthfully, it makes me feel like a bug under a microscope—like everyone is just waiting for me to do something a *leading lady* would do. I think that's why adults always say to me, "You're shyer than I thought you'd be!"—it's because they're expecting me to be more like Nana Rhea.

I'm definitely not.

Thankfully, Sadia and Tamzin actually like being the center of attention, so they take the spotlight pressure off me. They're very outgoing, so I bet they'll make lots of new friends at junior high. Which will be great! I think. I mean, hopefully once people become friends with Sadia and Tamzin, they'll become friends with me too, since we'll all be hanging out together. I'm pretty sure that's how it will work.

I sneak a quick glance at my parents in the crowd and see them both snapping photos on their phones. In the pictures I bet I look like a deer caught in headlights—not that I've ever *seen* a deer caught in headlights, but that's what Dad says to me anytime I'm forced to do something with people watching me. These better not be the photos that make our holiday card this year.

"Good luck next year, Audrey," Miss Rose says quietly when I reach her. She takes my hand, shakes it, and hands me my diploma.

"Thank you," I mumble before hurrying back to my place on stage.

I let out a relieved sigh when I make it back to my place in line beside Dylan and the audience switches their attention to the girl to my left, Caroline Dagwood.

And whoa. That was it. That was my last moment as a sixth grader.

I grip my diploma a little tighter. Is it just me, or does this graduation ceremony feel like it went by kind of fast?

Miss Rose calls out the rest of the names before officially pronouncing us Burbank Valley Elementary School graduates. The audience bursts into cheers, and everyone in my class rushes forward, trying to find their parents off stage.

I weave through the crowd to find my parents, feeling a bit lost in the sea of people. Since I haven't hit my growth spurt yet, it's hard for me to see over the tops of my classmates' heads. Thankfully, Dad spots me and tugs me over.

"Yay, Audrey!" Dad pulls me into a hug.

"Congratulations." Mom kisses the top of my head and smooths down some of my short, flyaway brown hair.

Dad holds up his phone. "I recorded the whole thing to show Nana Rhea tomorrow," he says. "She will be sad she missed it."

Nana Rhea lives about twenty minutes away in Hollywood and would usually come to things like this, but since she's moving houses tomorrow, Mom thought it was best for her to stay home and pack. Which, truthfully, was kind of a relief.

I love my Nana Rhea—don't get me wrong—but if she were here at my graduation, there'd be even *more* eyes on me. Plus, I don't need someone who used to perform for a living watching me sing the annoying graduation tune.

"Excuse me," says an unfamiliar voice from behind me.

I turn to see a tall woman with short, graying hair peering down at me with an excited grin.

"Sorry, but Rhea Covington is your grandmother, correct?" Her eyes light up as she stares at me.

I immediately shrink back. The hot and tingly feeling returns down my neck as I feel the attention spotlight turning on me. This woman is probably expecting me to give her a dazzling smile or show some great talent. I don't have either.

Mom steps forward and puts an arm around my shoulder. "If you don't mind, we're just enjoying the school graduation."

The woman gives an apologetic nod. "Of course, of course. Just wanted to say that I loved *Beauty in the Wind*. It was incredible. I wish Rhea Covington were still acting."

"Okay," Mom says, giving her a blank expression.

Unsure what to say next, the tall woman gives an awkward smile and walks off.

"Some people," Mom grumbles.

Dad squeezes Mom's arm.

I shake off the bad tingly feeling and look away from my parents to see Sadia and Tamzin, both still holding their diplomas, walking toward me. Sadia has long, shiny black hair with bangs cut straight across her forehead, and Tamzin has shoulder-length blond hair with a streak of it dyed hot pink. It looks *so* cool. I once asked Mom and Dad if I could dye my hair with a temporary streak—just to see how it looked—but they said the hair coloring had too many bad chemicals.

"We're officially seventh graders!" Sadia cheers when she reaches me.

"We are," I giggle.

"Let's walk to Deena's Ice Cream to celebrate," Tamzin suggests. "We could get double scoops!"

"Yes," Sadia agrees. "We deserve to get double scoops. *Seventh graders* get double scoops."

Sadia and Tamzin high-five, then look at me expectantly.

"Uhhh." I make a face. Deena's Ice Cream is more than a mile walk from here, and I'm not allowed to walk that far without an adult. "I'll have to ask my parents," I say.

Sadia rolls her eyes. It's the same look she gave me when I told her Mom and Dad wouldn't let me go to gymnastics camp with her. She's used to me saying stuff like this. Out of the three of us, my parents have the most rules, so it's not surprising that I have to ask their permission to do stuff my friends are allowed to do.

I turn to get Mom's attention. She's chatting with Dad. "Hey, Mom?" I tap her arm. "Can I walk to Deena's Ice Cream with my friends?"

Mom puts her hands on her hips and looks down. "By yourselves? Which adult is going with you?" She eyes the three of us.

"Umm..." I look over at my friends, and they shake their heads to signal that no adult is joining us. I snap my head back to Mom. "Just us," I say, trying to sound mature, independent, and very seventh-grader-y.

Mom frowns. "That's too far for you girls to walk on your own. Dad or I could come with you, though, if you really want to go."

I quickly glance back at my friends, but they're sharing an expression I can't really read. They don't exactly look happy with Mom's suggestion.

"Uh, no. That's okay," I answer.

"You sure?" Mom asks. "I don't mind driving you."

Out of the corner of my eye I see Sadia slowly shaking her head.

"No, thanks," I say quickly. If Tamzin and Sadia don't want to be driven by my parents, then neither do I.

"Okay," Mom says, shrugging, before going back to talking with Dad.

I turn to face my friends. Tamzin blows a strand of hair out of her face, and Sadia crosses her arms just like Dad.

"Want to walk somewhere closer?" I ask, hoping they aren't too disappointed by my suggestion.

"Like where?" Sadia raises an eyebrow.

"We could go hang out by the swings in the park," I try.

"I don't know," Tamzin sighs. "That seems a little... boring?"

I grimace. Tamzin has been saying this to me more and more. I want to leave *boring* behind in elementary school. I wish I had something more interesting to suggest—like playing video games or doing flips on a trampoline—but nothing comes to mind.

It was easier to come up with things to do when Sadia and Tamzin still liked hanging out in the neighborhood park. *I* still like hanging out in the park. At least I think I do. It's true we haven't actually done it in a while.

"Yeah," Sadia agrees. "And we used to do that in fifth grade. We're *seventh* graders now."

"Okay," I say, feeling sudden pressure to think of something better. "What if we went back to my house and watched a movie?"

"Your TV has those weird parental restrictions," says Sadia.

I tug at the sleeve around my wrist. "I just don't think I'm going to be able to talk my parents into letting me walk to Deena's without them. It is kind of far."

"Well, we're allowed to go," Tamzin says, sharing another look with Sadia. "Our parents don't think it's a far walk. We've done it before."

"Oh," I say, deflating. They've walked to Deena's

Ice Cream without me? When? Where was I? It's not like my family has gone anywhere recently. "You guys are going right now?" I ask, hoping they'll stay around a little bit longer to hang out while our parents all talk.

They look at each other and nod.

"Okay," I say, trying to put on a smile.

It's a little frustrating that my friends won't do something *I* can join in on too, but I don't want them to see that I'm disappointed—especially not so close to the sleepover. They might get irritated if they think I am upset, and I've seen the way Tamzin and Sadia argue with each other when they are annoyed. I always stay out of it. It's much easier to just be easygoing than to risk fighting with them. It's not worth ruining what we have over a little, *tiny* thing. Right?

"No worries," I say, putting on a pretend "I don't really mind" expression. "I probably have to do stuff with my parents later anyway. I'll see you tomorrow for the sleepover, though!" I give them a half-hearted smile.

They both smile back, but it looks sort of forced.

Sadia and Tamzin give me a wave before darting away through the crowd. I sigh as I watch them leave, wishing I was trailing after them.

At least I'll spend the entire day with them tomorrow.

Tomorrow everything will be fine. I'm sure of it.

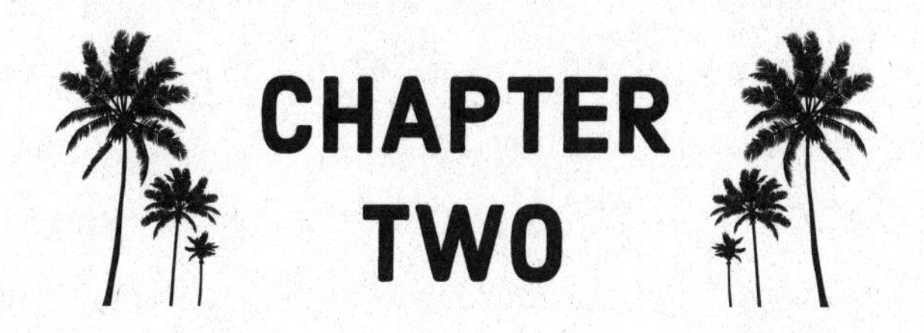

CHAPTER TWO

AS SOON AS my parents and I get home from graduation, I sprint to my room to start packing for the sleepover. I could pack in the morning, but I'm too excited to wait. Plus, I'm still feeling a little let down that my friends went to Deena's Ice Cream without me, and I think getting ready for tomorrow will take my mind off it.

Tamzin and Sadia probably—no, definitely—didn't mean to leave me behind. They did *want* me to come with them.

Unfortunately, just as I'm starting to feel a bit better, my parents come into my bedroom to rattle off their usual slumber-party rules. You'd think now that I'm a sixth-grade graduate, my parents would realize they don't have to go over all their rules before every sleepover. But nope. They don't.

"Still no PG-13 movies, Audrey. I know you're an elementary school graduate now, but that doesn't mean you're old enough to watch those yet," Mom says as I shove pajamas into the overnight bag on my bed. It's already stuffed with a sleeping bag, a swimsuit, fluffy socks, a phone charger, and a toothbrush.

"And no soda," Dad chimes in. "A couple of pieces of candy are fine, but soda has too much sugar. I was just reading an article about the effect soda can have on children's teeth."

I shove my hairbrush into a side pocket and nod without really paying attention. If Mom and Dad notice I'm in an unusually low mood, they don't ask why, which is perfectly fine with me. I wouldn't tell them why I was disappointed even if they *did* bring it up. Mom already thinks my friends don't have enough boundaries, and I don't want to have to defend them to her right now.

"Make sure Mrs. Harrison calls us if you girls end up leaving the house," Mom adds.

"Yeah, yeah, I *know*," I say as I try to zip up the overstuffed bag. My parents' sleepover rules have never changed. I could probably list them off in my sleep! And I've never broken any of them. My parents only let me go to sleepovers in the first place if I promise to follow their rules exactly. So even if I wanted to try staying up past ten (like Sadia and Tamzin are allowed to), I wouldn't want to risk my parents finding out and not letting me go again.

"Remember to text us right when you get there," Dad says, giving me a stern look.

I make a face and snap, "But I've been to Tamzin's a billion times!"

Dad crosses his arms and sighs. His gesture makes my shoulders rise up to my ears. Maybe I shouldn't have snapped at him. I *do* feel a little guilty now.

"Most accidents happen when kids are within three miles of their home," Dad says.

"Exactly," Mom says, nodding. She bites her lip. "On second thought, call us when you get there."

"Okay," I sigh, hoping this conversation ends soon so they get out of my room. There's no real point in arguing with them anyway—they never budge on relaxing their rules.

I want to text my friends to ask if there is anything else I should pack, but my parents will get grumpy if they see me staring at my phone while they're talking to me. They think that's rude.

"Good." Dad claps his hands together. "Well, we will leave you to it. I'll call up when dinner is ready."

"Mkay." I scan my room for anything else I should try to fit in my sleepover bag.

They head toward the door, but before they step out of my bedroom, Mom stops and says, "Oh, and Audrey?"

"Mhmm?" I look up at her.

"Congrats again on graduating sixth grade." She smiles.

I give her a half grin back, starting to feel a little better.

Mom walks out of my room right as I feel my phone buzz in my back pocket. I pull it out and swipe it open.

But when I read the text, hot sweat instantly coats my forehead.

I must be seeing this wrong. Or maybe I need glasses?

Yes, that must be it—I'm losing my eyesight. That, or my friends meant this message for someone else. There is no way *I'm* the person this text is supposed to be for.

I read it again.

> we don't think you should come
> to the sleepover tomorrow. no
> offense, but you can't do anything
> cool. maybe that sounds mean or
> whatever but you would understand
> if you were us. sorry.

The text is from Tamzin, but she's added Sadia to the chat.

I'm about to type a text back—something like, *I don't think you meant to send this to me haha*—when my phone buzzes again, and another text appears in the thread.

Yeah. Sorry, Audrey.

It's from Sadia.

A large lump forms at the back of my throat. I don't think my friends even know any other people named Audrey. Which means…this text really *is* meant for me.

I blink, and the words in the texts all start to jumble together.

I've been uninvited from our annual sleepover.

By my best friends.

On our graduation day.

Over text.

…

I let out a panicked giggle.

No. There's no way! There has to be some mistake. Or it's a joke. They would've said something at graduation if they planned to uninvite me, right?

I write back a message and quickly hit send.

What? I don't understand??? Is this a joke?

I stare at the screen until a third text comes through. It's from Sadia again.

Not a joke. There are some things we want to do now that we're technically in Jr High and we know you won't be allowed to do them. And we already decided what movie we want to watch tomorrow and if you come, we won't be able to see it.

My back stiffens.

A movie? *That's* what this is about? Yeah, okay, it's true my parents probably won't let me watch whatever they've picked out, but that doesn't mean I can't still come to the party. I could just do something else while they watch! That's an easy solution!

I quickly send a text back.

It's not a big deal. I don't have to see the movie. I can still come.

A few seconds later another text from Tamzin quickly lights up my screen.

> it's not just about the movie, you know? you're only allowed to do boring things. you can't even do the things we like to do.

Boring. There's that word again. Before I've had a chance to reply, there's another text from Sadia.

> Your parents are just too strict. We don't want their rules ruining our fun.

I stare at the words, reading them over and over.

There it is. The source of my problem: my parents and their rules. My friends want nothing to do with them.

I'm too stunned to look away from the phone. It feels like I've been punched in the gut.

Uninvited.

Bile rises into my mouth, and it tastes sour and thick. Tears well in my eyes, and I know if I blink, they'll run down my face. I want to write something back, but I'm not sure what to say.

Sorry about my parents?

Please let me come?

I'm going to show up tomorrow anyway whether you guys like it or not, and you'll just have to deal with it?

My fingers tremble as I type and delete several messages, but nothing feels right to send. The longer I stare at my phone, the tighter my throat gets. My chest heaves as I suck in air to keep myself from sobbing.

Okay, sure, I can't do all the same activities as them, but I thought we were all best friends! I thought we knew we *belonged* together. Don't they realize that if I don't go to this sleepover, I won't see them all summer? If I don't go tomorrow, the first time I'll see them again is when we start seventh grade!

Another terrible thought hits me.

Wait—do they...do they not want to hang out with me next year either? Have I just been completely dropped by my best friends?!

I suck in a breath.

If Sadia and Tamzin don't want me hanging out

with them in junior high, I'll be totally friendless! How am I supposed to make new friends when I don't really have anything in common with any other kids at school? My parents would *never* let me hang out with skateboarding-obsessed kids who spend all their free time at the skate park by the beach and always break their arms. And I doubt the super popular girls who already wear makeup to school would want me hanging around, especially since I can't even *try* makeup. And there is a zero percent chance I'll fit in with the drama kids who audition for every school musical—that's *way* too much spotlight for me.

But it's not like I play any sports or have any other interesting hobbies people might be into either! Whenever I've asked Mom or Dad to sign me up for a sports team, they've always had a reason to say no. And the *one* time I tried to convince them to let me play the drums, they said the instrument was way too loud, so they made me take snooze-worthy piano lessons instead! No one will want to be friends with me just because I can play a few old classical piano songs. The only cool thing about me is Nana Rhea, but even if people at school did care who she was, I don't want to be known only because of her. Then kids might expect me to be the life of the party and have amazing stories like *she* does.

I'll be a disappointment.

And I hate disappointing people.

I feel light-headed. I think I'm going to be sick. My breathing hitches as I reread the last text.

> Your parents are just too strict. We don't want their rules ruining our fun.

This doesn't feel real. How could Mom and Dad do this to me? They are making me the most boring person ever by not letting me do *anything* interesting!

As if my thoughts have summoned her, there's a knock on my door, and Mom pokes her head into my room.

"Audrey, I forgot to add—" She stops and frowns. "Are you okay?"

I use the back of my hands to quickly wipe my eyes.

"I'm *fine*," I snap, even though I'm definitely not fine. There's a horrible pressure on my lungs that feels like it's trying to push out all my breath.

Uninvited. Uninvited. Uninvited.

The word pounds over and over again in my head.

Mom steps into my bedroom. "What's wrong?"

I can't look her in the eye. I'm too mad.

"Sleepover is canceled," I try to say in my most normal-sounding voice. I don't want to tell her it's really only canceled for *me*. If Mom knew the truth, she'd probably get upset with Tamzin and Sadia. And Mom is not allowed to be upset with my friends. She'd probably call their parents and make everything worse. And besides, I don't want her pity. That'll make me feel even more terrible.

"Canceled?" She puts her hands on her hips. "That's odd. I spoke to Mrs. Harrison yesterday, and she was looking forward to having all you girls over. Maybe I'll call her and see—"

"No! Don't call," I shout, hot anger starting to bubble in my chest.

"Are you sure? I really think—"

Then, without meaning to, I blurt, "It's *your* fault!" Because she *did* ruin it, after all. If it weren't for my parents and all their rules, my friends wouldn't think I was boring and I'd still have a sleepover to go to! Mom and Dad practically forced my friends to ditch me. If my parents let me do all the things my friends wanted to do, this would have never happened!

My friends get to do things like get their ears pierced, dye their hair, and drink soda, but I'm not allowed to do any of that stuff. I don't even know if I *like* that stuff! So of course my friends don't want to spend time with me—my parents are holding me back!

Mom raises an eyebrow. "Wait, what?"

"You and Dad and all your rules made this happen! If it weren't for you, I'd still be going to the sleepover!"

Mom crosses her arms and narrows her eyes. "So it isn't canceled, but you no longer want to go . . . because of Dad and me?"

My hands ball at my sides and I admit through

clenched teeth, "I've been *uninvited*. My friends think you're too strict. And you know what? I wouldn't want to hang out with me either. When I'm around, my friends can't order pizza because you won't let me eat food with too much grease, or go shopping in the teen section because you won't let me buy anything too '*mature*,' or—or—or tons of other things!"

She looks at me, stunned. She's not used to me acting like this. *I'm* not used to me acting like this. But tonight Mom definitely deserves it.

"Ah, I see," she says, shifting her weight and starting to tap her toe against my bedroom carpet. "I'm the bad guy here."

"Clearly!" I loudly scoff.

Mom scrunches her eyebrows together. "Where is this new attitude coming from?"

I stare down at the floor so I don't have to look at her expression. It'll only make me feel ashamed for raising my voice, and I don't want to feel like that right now. I want to be mad.

"I'm sorry your friends are acting this way," Mom continues, "but I'm not going to apologize for keeping you safe and healthy." She sighs. "I know I don't talk about my childhood very often, but when I was a kid, *my* mom—"

I cut her off. "I don't care. This is my life, Mom. Not yours!"

"All right," she says, backing away. "You're obviously worked up, so I'm going to let you simmer down. You can come out when dinner is ready."

I look up from my hands. "I don't need to simmer down. I—!"

But before I can finish, Mom closes the door behind her.

I seethe as I stare at the back of my now-shut door, fury still pumping through my body. I wish I could chuck my overnight bag out the window and wrench open my bedroom door just so I can slam it closed again.

Uninvited.

It takes a few seconds for my breathing to return to normal. When it does, I slump onto my bed with a scowl, trying to think of any way to make this better.

I really have only one option—I need to somehow

get re-invited to the sleepover and prove to my friends that I still belong with them. If I don't, I'll have zero friends and be all alone in junior high. That'll be so embarrassing!

Maybe if I can show my friends that I don't *only* do boring things, they'll want me back!

But how do I do that?

I rest my face between my palms and think, hoping some brilliant idea of how to win my friends back jumps out at me. There has to be something I can do. But what? There's not much I can do between now and tomorrow morning.

Is there?

I furrow my brows and rack my brain for an answer. No plan comes to mind. And the longer I sit, the more upset with my parents I get. I get mad about them saying no about gymnastics camp, and for saying no to drum lessons, and for not letting me dye my hair, and for not letting me stay up late, and for, well, *everything*.

It all just makes me mad, mad, mad.

A few hours later, Dad calls me for dinner, but even

though my stomach gurgles, I don't go out and join them. I don't even want to look at them.

So for the rest of the night, I angrily stew alone in my room. What an amazing way to spend the first night of summer.

Not.

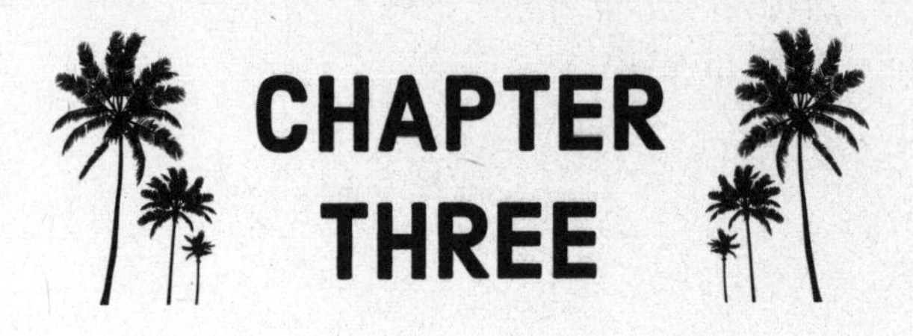

CHAPTER THREE

"I KNOW YOU'RE upset, but you can't spend all day here by yourself while Dad and I are at Nana Rhea's helping her move. You need to get dressed," Mom says when she walks into the kitchen the next morning.

I'm hunched over the kitchen table and frowning at my frustratingly healthy breakfast. At Tamzin's house, there's an entire selection of breakfast options and none of them are *bland* or *whole grain*.

I use my spoon to lift a bite of my lumpy oatmeal,

glare at it, then tilt the spoon to let it drop back into the bowl with a plop. Soggy oats spatter onto the kitchen table, and Mom shoots me a "you better clean that up" look, so I grab a napkin and wipe it away with a frown.

"Why can't I spend the day here? I'm almost *twelve*. I'm not about to set the house on fire or anything," I sneer.

I've already decided I'll be spending this entire day just as mad as I was last night. Since I couldn't come up with any plan that would get my friends to re-invite me, there is no possible way for me to enjoy this day. Not while knowing the annual sleepover is happening without me.

"Audrey," Mom sighs. "We're not arguing about this. You know you're not allowed to spend more than an hour here by yourself. It's a safety thing. Now get dressed so we get to Nana Rhea's on time."

I groan, stand from my chair, and dump the rest of my oatmeal into the sink. Mom gives me her disapproving look as I stomp out of the kitchen and toward my bedroom to change.

I do feel kind of bad for arguing with her, but right now I'm still too irritated to let it go.

Mom probably expects me to wear something nice and matching to Nana Rhea's. But I will not. If I have to go spend the day with my parents, I'm going to wear my old oversized hoodie with holes in the sleeves that Mom dislikes.

After I tug on old jeans, a gray T-shirt, and the hoodie, I reluctantly trudge back into the kitchen and find my parents discussing the boring details of Nana Rhea's move.

Basically, years and years ago, Nana Rhea used to live with Mom's dad, but he moved to Europe while Mom and her sister, my auntie Gwen, were still young, because he wanted to be an artsy director instead of a father—at least that's what Mom told me. I've never met him and don't really think of him as my grandpa. For as long as I've been alive, Nana Rhea has lived in her Hollywood house all by herself.

However, when the fiftieth anniversary of *Beauty in the Wind* happened earlier this year, the media ran a whole bunch of "Where is she now?" stories on Nana

Rhea and accidentally leaked her address online, so fans and paparazzi started showing up there to sneak photos. Ever since, Mom and Auntie Gwen have been trying to talk Nana Rhea into moving to some private luxury retirement community for her safety.

Nana Rhea was totally against the idea of moving until one of the paparazzi tried to break into her house to take a photo of her wardrobe. Mom and Auntie Gwen got even more concerned about their mom living in a house all by herself, so they pestered her about it until she finally gave in and agreed to move *for their sake*.

Since Auntie Gwen lives across the country, Mom and Dad organized the whole thing themselves. They've been blabbing about moving vans and protective coverings and packing and all that stuff for weeks. To be honest, I never really paid that much attention. I always thought I'd be at the annual sleepover today, so there was no need for me to care about my parents' plans for Nana Rhea's move.

The thought makes a lump form in my throat again. I choke it down as my parents stop talking and eye my outfit. Mom looks like she might say something about my old sweatshirt, but she doesn't. I almost kind of wish she would so I could give her a snappy response back. No idea what snappy response I would actually come up with, though. It's not like I have a lot of them saved up, since I always stay out of arguments between my friends, and I don't usually talk back to my parents. But maybe having a few snappy comebacks would help me seem more interesting.

Mom pulls her phone out from her purse on the table to look at the time. "We should go. I want to get there before the moving van arrives in case there are any last-minute boxes Nana Rhea needs help packing."

Dad gives a quick nod, takes one last sip of his coffee, and goes to grab the car keys. I pat my front hoodie pocket to make sure I've got my phone. I do.

If I were still going to the sleepover, I'd probably be sending off a text right now letting Tamzin know I was about to walk over to her house. I wonder if Sadia is already there. If she is, have the two of them posted any photos together yet?

With gut-tightening curiosity, I pull out my phone to check if any of them have posted anything on their social accounts.

But they haven't. There are no posts or photos I haven't already seen.

I'm not sure if that makes me feel better or worse. On the one hand, I kind of do want to see what I'm missing out on, but on the other, I want to pretend the sleepover was canceled for them too—not just me.

I tuck my phone back into my pocket just as Dad tells me to load into the car. Knowing there is nothing I can say or do to keep me from going with them, I reluctantly trudge after him.

"Nana Rhea will be happy to see you," Dad says as he backs the car out of the garage and takes off down the road.

He's such a slow driver. Mom always likes to tell the story about their first road trip together. Apparently, when she found out Dad drove five miles under the speed limit, she realized she was in love with him. I guess it's because Nana Rhea used to drive Mom and

Auntie Gwen around town like a race car driver, so it was the first time Mom had felt safe in a car.

I think Mom's being a bit dramatic. I've never seen Nana Rhea behind the wheel, but I doubt Nana Rhea's driving is *that* bad. Or this slow.

I look out my window and picture myself running next to the car. I bet I could sprint faster than we're going. At this rate, we won't get to Nana Rhea's until next week.

"Mhmm," I answer, still staring out the window.

Mom turns around in her seat to look at me. "I get that you're in a bad mood and you didn't expect to come with us to Nana Rhea's today, but please, when we get there, be helpful and don't make this day any harder than it needs to be. Moving is stressful for everyone."

"Can't I just wait in the car?"

"No, you're going to help us bring boxes out and into the moving van. The sooner we get this move done, the sooner we can all relax."

I lean my head back against the headrest.

Maybe Sadia and Tamzin are already changing into

their suits to go for a morning swim in Tamzin's pool. Not sure why I couldn't be there for something like *that*. I am allowed to go swimming—while grown-ups are present.

I look back out the window and try to think of all the cool things they may be doing that my parents would never allow. Maybe they're dyeing their hair new colors or watching a PG-13 movie.

Ugh.

It really stinks having strict parents.

Twenty minutes later, Dad switches on the blinker to indicate for the next exit, and we practically move in slo-mo as the car heads off the freeway and up onto the steep and winding street that leads to Nana Rhea's neighborhood. The twisty road is lined with cliff-hugging houses, shiny cars, and tall palm trees. It's the type of place you'd see on a postcard for the Hollywood Hills.

Dad slows the car even more as we go around the turns, giving me time to pick out landmarks I recognize from above. I'm pretty sure I can see the park where I had my fourth-birthday party. And the cluster of the glass buildings downtown where my doctor's office is. And the street with all the colorful thrift shops Mom once took me to.

Tamzin loves thrift shopping. I should tell her about that street. Maybe she and I…

My chest constricts when I think about my friend's texts again.

> you're only allowed to do boring things. you can't even do the things we like to do.

Maybe Tamzin would think thrift shopping with me would be too boring now.

I shift my weight in my seat. I want to check for new posts from Sadia or Tamzin, but just as I reach for my phone, Dad pulls into Nana Rhea's driveway.

Nana Rhea's house doesn't look like much from the front. There are a couple of palm trees by the main door, a cracked concrete driveway that leads to a tan-colored garage, and red tiles on the roof that hang over the sides of the building. You'd never guess that on the inside, Nana Rhea's house is like a giant museum, filled with paintings, sculptures, books, and millions of other various things.

We climb out of the car, and Mom knocks on the door. There's the sound of movement from somewhere inside.

Dad leans closer to me and says in a hushed tone, "Be careful inside, Audrey."

I don't respond. He says this to me every time we come here. It's not like I'm going to walk inside and smash one of Nana Rhea's sculptures.

"Don't worry," Mom says, patting Dad's arm. "Everything should be packed already. I told my mom to box up the last things yesterday. I'm sure nothing too breakable will still be out. Let's just be quick to start getting the boxes outside and—"

The door swings open, revealing Nana Rhea smiling out at us and not wearing something I would call a "moving outfit." She's got on fluffy slippers and a thick quilted robe over blue pajamas. It does, however, look like she's put on some makeup. She has on light-pink lipstick and brown mascara, and her short blond hair is pulled back in a jewel-studded clip. Even while wearing slippers and a robe, she gives off a sense of elegance and confidence. Suddenly, I do feel a bit awkward wearing my old sweatshirt.

Nana Rhea catches my eye. "Audrey!" She leans forward to give me a hug. "Congrats on graduating elementary school, dear."

"Hi, Nana Rhea," I say, doing my best to plaster on a smile. I'm not *not* happy to see my grandma, of course, but my chest still feels tight from thinking about the sleepover. I shouldn't even be at Nana Rhea's house. I should be at Tamzin's, enjoying my friends and not questioning if I'll be a loner next year.

Nana Rhea smooths her hand down the side of my hair. "My sweet, don't slouch. Exude the confidence you have."

My smile drops into a frown when Nana Rhea looks over at Mom. What confidence does she want me to show?

Mom narrows her eyes at Nana Rhea's outfit. "Mom, you're not even dressed. The movers will be here soon."

Nana Rhea crosses her arms. "Well, you didn't call. I wasn't sure what time to expect you."

Mom raises an eyebrow. "I sent you an email about the plan for today last week. I told you we'd be coming around now."

Nana Rhea rubs Mom's arm. "Oh, honey, you know I don't really read my emails."

"You responded to it."

Nana Rhea makes a waving gesture with her hand and walks back into her house without responding. Then she calls over her shoulder, "Come in, come in!"

I'm expecting to see stacks of packed boxes when we enter the living room, but instead, the room looks like it always does. There's a large white couch and long wooden coffee table next to two sliding glass doors that lead out to a city-overlooking balcony. Art, family photos, and old posters of her films decorate the main room, and colorful books neatly line a massive bookcase. A hallway on the right leads to the kitchen, and stairs to the left go to the bedrooms. The only thing that looks out of place is the stack of empty boxes near the side of the room.

Mom looks around the house with a tight-lipped expression. "Mom, didn't you say you were already going to be boxed up by the time we got here? What were you doing all day yesterday? The moving van will be here in an hour."

"Pack everything by *myself*? Don't be silly. It's too much. But I did box up some old photo albums yesterday." She motions to a tiny box shoved into the corner.

"But, *Mom*, that's why we asked you if you needed our packing help. You said no. We could've come by during the week and helped you get all this done."

"I didn't want to make you guys do that. I thought that's why we hired people to help me move."

Mom puts her hands on her hips. "Those are movers, not packers."

"Then we should've hired packers. It's not like we can't afford it." Nana Rhea shrugs.

"Why would we hire someone to do something we can do? That's not sensible. You know I don't like spending money unnecessarily."

"And you know *I* do." Nana Rhea grins.

"Yes, but now..." Mom stops, closes her eyes, and

takes a deep breath. "It's fine. What's done is done. We don't have time for the back-and-forth. We'll just have to hurry and pack up what we can now."

"Oh, that's so sweet of you. Thank you." Nana Rhea smiles. "I'll go make us some tea."

"No, Mom. Don't—we need to—"

But Nana Rhea has already swept out of the room, leaving Mom, Dad, and me alone in the very un-packed living room.

Mom sighs and mutters to herself, "Not sure how I didn't see this coming. Should've known this place wouldn't be packed. This is so like her." She looks at me. "Audrey, can you grab a box and see if Nana Rhea has started packing any of the bedrooms? If not, can you pack away grandma's closet? We can come back later for stuff in the other bedrooms if necessary, but her clothes are important to get boxed up."

"Me?" I groan.

Mom gives me a death glare.

"Fine, fine," I mumble as I grab an empty box and drag it behind me toward Nana Rhea's bedroom. Hiring packers does seem like it would've been a lot easier for everyone. Why does Mom always have to do the *sensible* thing?

At least if I'm in the closet by myself, my parents won't be able to bother me or give me more things to do. I guess I only ever do what my parents want me to anyway. It's true that they've basically always picked my activities for me.

But...

What things would I even want to do if I *did* have the choice?

Right now I'd choose just to go back home.

Maybe my friends were right. Maybe my parents *have* doomed me to be dull. Just look at me now, dragging an empty box at my grandma's house. I mean, I couldn't even think of a way to prove to them I was interesting. Clearly that must mean something.

I hurry upstairs before I start tearing up again. Nana Rhea's room is the last door at the end of the hall, so as I walk toward it, I peer into the first few rooms to see if any of them are packed up. They're not. At all.

I push open the door to Nana Rhea's bedroom. Inside, there is a large canopy bed with too many pillows, five floor-to-ceiling windows that look out over Los Angeles, and an en suite bathroom. As expected, nothing is packed. There are zero signs that Nana Rhea won't be living here anymore.

I roll my eyes, head into the walk-in closet beside the bathroom entrance, and flick on the light. My eyes squint as they adjust to the brightness, and I blink as I look around. All of Nana Rhea's clothes are still hanging neatly in color-coordinated rows.

Still sad and not ready to tackle packing, I toss aside the empty box and slide my back down the closet wall to a comfortable sitting position. I bring my knees to my chest and pull my phone out of my sweatshirt pocket to scroll through it and check for new posts.

And... there is something new. A photo posted by Tamzin eight minutes ago. In the picture my friends are smiling and wearing cute two-piece bathing suits next to the pool.

Groan.

My parents only buy me one-piece bathing suits because they don't want me getting too "sun exposed." I once asked if I could try a two-piece suit, but all that led to was Mom and Dad lecturing me about sunscreen and proper skin protection.

I stare at the photo.

How long have my friends been wanting to do things without me? Have my parents' rules *always* held them back? Was Deena's Ice Cream the final straw?

I sniff back tears.

"Hiding away, are we?"

I jump to my feet, wipe my nose, and look up to see Nana Rhea holding a pink teacup in her hand and smirking at me.

"No, I, uh, I'm packing your closet," I say as I quickly pull a silk shirt off its hanger, fold it, and put it into the box.

"Oh, Audrey, not like that," Nana Rhea tuts. She takes the shirt back out of the box and refolds it over her arm with one hand before carefully placing it back down.

My lips curl into a grimace. Great, apparently folding has rules too.

"You know," Nana Rhea says, pulling another shirt off a hanger and looking fondly at it, "I bought this shirt in Morocco when I was filming the movie *Beauty in the Wind*. This shirt is practically a collectible."

"Cool." I nod, not exactly sure what to say.

She pulls out a pair of sequined pants. "And I bought these in Las Vegas, back when I was choosing all the wrong activities but all the *right* outfits."

I raise an eyebrow. *Wrong activities*? I don't think I've heard *those* stories before. Mom definitely hasn't shared them with me.

Her comment makes my mind return to its previous thought—what kind of stuff would I choose to do if I could? In Mom and Dad's opinion, I bet all my choices would be considered the wrong activities too. At least that's what they thought about the drums, the hair dye, and simply walking to Deena's.

"And this!" She holds up a fancy, old-fashioned dress, pulling me from my thoughts. "Well, I shouldn't really tell you about the night I wore this."

That gets my full attention.

"No, tell me," I encourage.

She leans forward and whispers, "I ditched a magazine interview to go to a yacht party in the south of Italy." Nana Rhea winks. "I used to love parties on boats." But then her voice changes as she says, almost sadly, "That was before I stopped acting, of course." She hangs the dress back up.

Wanting to hear more interesting stories, I point to a long, embroidered leather jacket. "What about that?"

"Now that," she says while reaching for the hanger, "was given to me by the lead singer of the band Elbow Grease. Have you ever heard of them?"

I shake my head no, captivated. Mom never really shares much about Nana Rhea's fame.

"Probably for the best."

"But what about—"

"Mom?" my mom shouts from another room. "Can you please come tell me if I can throw these old magazines out?"

Nana Rhea sighs. "It seems I'm needed in the other room to supervise." She hands me the hanger with the leather jacket and glances around the closet. "Please be careful when boxing this all up, Audrey."

I try not to make a face or mention that she could

have already packed this all up the way she wanted by *herself*.

"I will," I mumble.

Nana Rhea smiles before exiting the closet, leaving me alone to box up her things and wonder all about what wrong activities I'd choose, given the opportunity.

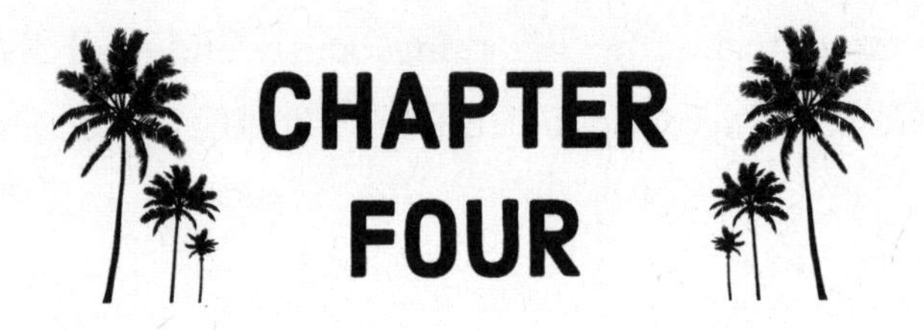

CHAPTER FOUR

THE MOVING VAN arrives at exactly twelve o'clock. When we hear its tires roll into the driveway, Mom and Dad start frantically taping up boxes and muttering about how many things still need to be packed away. We've only managed to box up Nana Rhea's room, a bathroom, some of the living room, and the cupboards in the kitchen. It's a whirlwind.

I'm so hot from all the packing that I have to take off my hoodie. Mom and Dad look sweaty too. Their cheeks are flushed from carrying and packing Nana

Rhea's heavy stuff. Nana Rhea, on the other hand, doesn't look uncomfortable at all. She's changed into a cream-colored shirt, light-blue pants, and a shawl. I have no idea when she had time to do her hair, but it's been blow-dried to sit just above her ears in loose curls.

When the professional movers march into the house, Nana Rhea tries to instruct them on how to carry out the big items, but Mom asks her to *please* be quiet and let them do their job in peace.

It takes around two hours to get the moving van loaded with the packed boxes. In a defeated tone, Mom tells the professional movers not to worry about grabbing everything else in the house because she's going to have to book them to come again anyway.

By the time we're ready to leave Nana Rhea's for the retirement community, I'm so hungry, I'd chow down anything, even if it was bland or whole grain.

"We'll get something to eat once we're at Nana Rhea's new place," Mom says for the hundredth time after I moan about my rumbling stomach. "We didn't expect to be here this long."

When we're ready to go, Nana Rhea and I buckle ourselves into the back seat of my parents' car and follow the moving van down the winding road and into the city. Nana Rhea's smiles from the closet are long gone. Instead, she stares out her window with a gloomy expression. I don't blame her. I didn't want to leave my house today either.

Then again, Mom and Auntie Gwen are kind of right about her safety. Nana Rhea lives all alone. What if some obsessed stalker-fan really does come into her house after finding her address online? Or what if more paparazzi try to break in? Besides, if Nana Rhea really didn't want to move, she could've said no. Unlike me, *she* has that privilege. I mean, sure, Mom and Auntie Gwen did bug her about it a lot, but Nana Rhea agreed. She's not being forced to move. She's just being unhelpful.

"There it is." Dad points out the windshield once we're down the hill and driving through the city.

I follow his gaze and—*whoa*—Nana Rhea's new home looks like a huge, swanky hotel. Behind a sign that reads **SEABREEZE PALMS, LUXURY LIVING COMMUNITY**, there is a three-tiered fountain out front, perfectly cut lawns, and—is that a valet service? Jeez, this place is nice.

I glance over to Nana Rhea, but she still doesn't look impressed. I guess, as a movie star, she's probably seen fancier buildings.

We follow the moving van around a circular drive and come to a stop right in front of the Seabreeze Palms entrance. A smiling person in a green uniform races out of the building to open our doors.

"You can leave your keys in the car, sir," the uniformed person says to Dad. "I'll park it in our private lot. When you need your car back, come to the valet desk for your keys."

Dad looks impressed. "Thanks!"

"No problem. Entrance is right through there." They point toward a tiled staircase.

We follow their directions into the luxurious building.

"Welcome, welcome, welcome!" a tall man with long, blond hair pulled into a low ponytail greets us enthusiastically after we step through automatic doors.

His eyes sparkle with delight when he sees Nana Rhea. "Wow. Rhea Covington, *the* Rhea Covington," he says in awe as he shakes Nana Rhea's hand. "Welcome to Seabreeze Palms. We're so excited to have you here. I'm Arnold, the community director."

Nana Rhea flings her shawl over one shoulder. "Nice you meet you, Arnold. This is my daughter Kendra, and my son-in-law Eric, and my granddaughter Audrey."

Arnold bounces with excited energy. "The whole family! A pleasure."

Mom and Dad shake his hand.

"Should we have the movers leave the van where it is outside?" Dad asks, motioning his thumb over his shoulder.

Arnold nods. "Yes, that's perfect. Our expert Seabreeze Palms staff will start moving everything into your villa while I give you the tour." He beckons us forward. "You're going to love it here."

"For the price, I should be absolutely *enthralled* by it." Nana Rhea gives him a small smile.

Arnold momentarily falters, but when he sees Nana

Rhea's smile, he laughs, thinking she's joking. I don't think she is.

"Gosh, it really is a pleasure to have you here," he says, beaming at her. "All right, now follow me toward the atrium, the first stop on our tour!"

Arnold bounces on his toes as he leads us around the place, and Mom, Dad, and Nana Rhea ask lots of snooze-worthy questions. I tune the whole thing out and shove my hands into my sweatshirt pocket to feel my phone. I really want to pull it out and scroll my feed again to see if my friends have posted any more photos, but I figure it's safer to wait until the tour is over. My parents might take my phone away if they think I'm being rude to Arnold for not listening to him. I have no idea why they'd expect me to care about this tour in the first place, but it's better to be safe than sorry in case they do.

After what seems like an eternity of walking, we're led to Nana Rhea's new home. The door is already propped open as people carry her boxes inside from the moving van.

"We can set up the place however you'd like it," Arnold says to Nana Rhea.

"Thank you." She gives him another smile, but it seems a little off. Usually when she's out in public, Nana Rhea goes full celebrity and gives everyone wide, dazzling grins. Maybe she's tired.

"And that's the end of the tour! Have any more questions for me?" Arnold beams.

"Actually," Mom says as she steps forward, "we're all pretty hungry. I was wondering if there is anywhere close by to go eat?"

Arnold claps his hands together. "Yes! Right across the street there are tons of great options. Don't even need to drive! You can walk right over."

Mom looks at Dad. "I'm thinking we should go grab some food and bring it back over here. Then when we're done eating, we can help with setting up."

Before Dad has a chance to answer, Arnold adds, "You're welcome to eat in our sunroom while they're still moving stuff into the villa."

"Yes, let's do that," Mom says with a nod. "Mom? Audrey? Why don't you two stay here in case the movers have any questions about anything, and Dad and I will be right back with some food."

"Sure." I shrug. I'm open to any plan that involves eating at this point.

"Don't get anything fried." Nana Rhea makes a face. "And I don't particularly care for anything that comes wrapped in greasy paper."

"Yes, Mom. I've been alive for forty-three years. I know what you like to eat," Mom says.

Nana Rhea gives her an approving nod.

"Don't worry," I tell Nana Rhea with an edge to my voice. "Mom has never bought me anything fried."

Nana Rhea raises an eyebrow. "Not even just to try?"

"I'm not buying her that stuff," Mom says defensively. "No nutritional value."

Nana Rhea opens her mouth to say something back, but Mom claps her hands together and says, "All right. Why don't you two follow Arnold to the sunroom, and we will be right back. Okay?"

"Okay," I mumble.

Arnold looks happy to have another job involving Nana Rhea. As Mom and Dad head back toward the front of the building, Arnold leads us in the opposite direction, pointing out more things as we go—"That hallway leads to a pool!" and "Mail services are through there!"

I hope my parents bring back something tasty—something like a huge sandwich or an extra-large burrito. My stomach rumbles just *thinking* about a delicious burrito.

It rumbles again. But this time, it feels a little strange. It almost feels like...

My phone is buzzing in my front pocket!

I shove my hand into my pocket, but before I can pull it out and see my new notification, I hear Nana Rhea ask, "Did you hear me, Audrey?"

I snap my attention to her. "What?" I must've tuned her out when my phone buzzed.

"I *said*, I think I need some time to decompress in my new place. This move is a lot all at once. Why don't you stay with Arnold and have him lead you to the sunroom?"

"Our staff is probably still bringing your boxes into the villa," Arnold interjects.

"That's okay." She smiles. "It'd just be great to get a feel for the rooms."

"Sure," I say. "I'll stay with Arnold."

Then a thought bubbles into my mind. I don't want to look at my phone in front of Arnold. I don't even really *know* him! What if the notification is not what I hope it is and I start to tear up again? I'll look pathetic if it seems like I'm crying because my grandma left me. I need to read this somewhere private—somewhere I can read and reread whatever this text says without him hovering over my shoulder.

"I'll meet you two in the sunroom, okay?" Nana Rhea says.

"Um, okay," I say, distracted.

She pats my shoulder before heading back down the hall toward her new place.

As I watch her walk away, I get a lightbulb idea. There is *one* place I can read my message while totally alone. All I need to do is get there and back before Nana Rhea meets us for lunch. And I also don't want Arnold following me. That wouldn't help anything.

I know I shouldn't lie—and I rarely ever do—but desperate times call for desperate measures. The only problem is, I've never been good at bending the truth. In fact, I'm pretty sure I'm the worst liar in the world. When I've tried it before, my voice shakes and I can't look the other person in the eye. But unfortunately, in order to read this notification alone, I'll have to tell a *tiny* white lie.

"Actually, I, uh, think I need to, um, go to the bathroom," I tell Arnold, looking down at my feet.

"It's just around that corner," he says, pointing. "I'll wait for you here!"

His instantly trusting response almost throws me off. Although I guess it *is* a very believable lie.

But I'm definitely *not* going to the bathroom. There is too high of a chance that someone could come in and hear me crying in a stall. No, I need to be completely alone.

I head in the direction Arnold pointed. When I turn the corner, I speed-walk as fast as I can past the bathroom door and back out the automatic doors. When I see the valet desk, I skid to a halt. The person in a green uniform raises their eyebrow at me.

It takes me a moment to catch my breath, and I'm

still panting when I ask, "Can I have the keys to that blue car that drove in not that long ago?"

The uniformed person blinks at me. "No," they say with a chuckle.

I furrow my brow. "Why not?" I ask, a little surprised with myself. Usually, I would just accept the *no* and move on, but reading this message is too important. It could change everything. It could mean not losing my friends.

"Because you're not sixteen and that is not your car."

I huff out an annoyed breath. "It's my *parents'* car."

They eye me suspiciously. "Even so, Seabreeze Palms policy says I can't hand you the keys. Sorry."

My phone feels like a heavy weight in my hand. The text is just waiting there, unread and unanswered. There has to be something I can say to get the keys from this person. Something that will make them…

I get another lightbulb idea.

What's one more teeny-tiny lie? It worked well with Arnold, so maybe I can bend the truth again and get the keys to the car.

The person looks at me curiously, probably wondering why I'm still standing here. If I'm going to go through with my idea, I better do it fast before I lose my nerve. Besides, I need to be quick since Arnold is waiting.

For a second time, I awkwardly look down at my feet as my pulse doubles in speed.

"Well, actually, my family is moving my Nana Rhea—*Rhea Covington*—in here today, and I'm actually, um, doing her a favor by grabbing a sweater *she* left in the car," I say.

I have no idea what made me think of that lie, but it does sound like it could be true. And as much as I don't like being known just for being related to Nana Rhea, today I think it'll work in my favor. Besides, it's only a small lie, I guess. We really are moving her in. She just didn't leave anything in the back seat.

Their eyes widen in surprise. "The actress Rhea Covington? I thought that was her walking inside, but I wasn't sure. So it's true? It was her?"

I fight back a smile. My shaking voice did not give me away!

I clear my throat before continuing my fake story. "Oh, yes. And, um, she's really tired from moving, so she didn't want to come *all* the way back out to the car. But I guess if you can't give me the keys, I'll go let her know and—"

"Here!" The uniformed person thrusts the car keys into my hand. "I get it. It is really tiring to move. And can you, uh, tell her I really admire her old stuff? I wish there were more of it. I'm an aspiring actor myself."

I stare down at the keys in my hand.

Oh. That worked.

"Sure!" I tell them. Before they have a chance to ask me more questions, I quickly add, "And thanks!" Then I hurry toward the private parking lot. I do feel a little bad for tricking them, but I need some time to myself without any interruptions!

When I spot our car in the lot, I hustle over and fumble with the keys to unlock it. I slide into the back seat and quickly shut the door behind me. Since I don't want anyone to see me randomly sitting in an empty parked car and come over to investigate, I lie down across the seat so that my head is lower than the window.

I'm finally alone.

I swipe open my phone and immediately click the message notification. A text opens and my eyes scan over it before I can actually take in what it says. I take a deep breath and read it slower.

> Hi Audrey! It's Auntie Gwen.
> Forgot to reach out yesterday to
> congratulate you on graduating sixth
> grade. Hope to see you soon! Kiss,
> Auntie Gwen.

The text is so unexpected, it takes me a second to even understand it.

Auntie Gwen?? What the heck?!

This isn't the text I wanted my phone to buzz with. Why did Auntie Gwen have to send me a message *now*? Where is the text from one of my friends? Where is the message where they beg me to rejoin the sleepover?

I groan and close out the text without replying. Auntie Gwen has horrible timing.

I close my eyes and slowly let out a long breath. There's a tight pressure in my chest again, so I cross my arms around my middle. Unfortunately, when I shut my eyes, all I see are visions of my friends hanging out without me, which makes the lump in my throat come back.

This text letdown feels almost worse than yesterday's because—at least for a moment—I had hope. Hope that I was back in with my friends and that this was all just some big misunderstanding. Hope that I could put this day behind me and still have my friend group.

I squeeze my arms around my stomach.

I'd never given it too much thought before yesterday, but I do wish I could try more cool things like Sadia and Tamzin do. I've always known my parents are stricter than most, but it has never ruined my social life like *this*. It has always seemed like my friends were okay with the way things were.

But for the first time, I'm realizing just how much I've been missing out on. When Mom and Dad had said no to *one* thing, it hadn't seemed like the end of the world. But now looking back on everything they've held me back from...it feels like a lot. More than I realized.

What if I would've really enjoyed something they've said no to? What if video games, or drums, or gymnastics, or something else I've never done could be my "calling"?

I don't even really *know* what I like.

Sigh.

Maybe *I'm* not okay with the way things were.

I flip over to my side, making my knees uncomfortably push against the back of the seat. My arms are sore from carrying boxes, and I didn't sleep too well last night. It hits me just how tired I am.

Tired, upset, and hungry. I know I should probably head back inside so Arnold doesn't wonder where I am, but I can't bring myself to sit up.

I wish things were different. I wish I had more choices and I wish I'd come up with a plan to make my friends take me back. But I don't and I didn't.

My breathing slows as I let the worn-out feeling spread through my body. I could nap here. Just for a minute or two.

I yawn. The tiredness starts to take over...

...

...

I feel another buzzing sensation, but I don't bother to check my phone this time. I know I'll just be disappointed when it's Auntie Gwen again.

The buzzing starts again. Only, I guess it's not *just* buzzing. It feels like low full-body rumble. And it's getting stronger. In fact, the seat beneath me is shaking. But that can't be right, can it? Phones can't make vibrations that big.

I open my eyes with a start, sensing something is off.

It's not my phone buzzing—it's the *car* rumbling. It's moving. The car is actually moving! I must've drifted asleep for a moment and didn't hear my parents start the car. But why are we driving away from Nana Rhea's new place? And where are we going?

I lift myself into a sitting position to ask Dad what's going on.

But when I see who is gripping the wheel, I gasp.

"Nana Rhea?!" I shriek. "What are you doing?!"

Nana Rhea jumps in her seat and swivels her head around to look at me. "Audrey?! What are you doing back there? You're supposed to be with Arnold!"

We're pulling out of the parking lot, then flying down the road at an incredible speed. I quickly grab the seat belt and buckle myself in, just in time for Nana Rhea to spin the wheel, and the car lurches over to the left as we take the next turn.

"Me?" I exclaim, still gripping tight to the seat belt across my chest. What are *you* doing? You're supposed to be decompressing. And should you even be driving?!"

As if answering my question, Nana Rhea crosses over the center divider and heads straight for a giant tree. The car picks up speed as the tree gets closer and closer.

"Watch out!" I shout.

Nana Rhea swerves to miss hitting the trunk but hits a mailbox instead. Letters and splinters of wood bounce off the hood of the car. We bump along the sidewalk before careening back into the street.

"That mailbox came out of nowhere," Nana Rhea huffs under her breath.

"I think you should pull over!" I say as we take another tight corner turn. My head smacks against the window.

"No, I'm getting the hang of it now," she insists. "It's just been a while!"

I've never seen Nana Rhea drive, so I don't doubt *that* one bit. Although I do doubt that it was ever legal to take up two lanes.

"People are honking at us!" I look behind me to see the angry faces of the people we're cutting off as we weave our way down the street.

"Let them honk." She waves me off with a flick of her wrist, and we start veering toward oncoming traffic.

I scream. Thankfully, Nana Rhea corrects our path just in time.

We're driving so fast, the cars we pass only look like streaks of color.

"Where are we going?!" I ask. "We really need to go back. Mom and Dad will be bringing the food to the sunroom soon and expect to see us!"

"Oh, I can't go back there, darling." She bites her bottom lip. "Not yet."

Another swerve, more screeching tires.

"What?!" I holler. "But we need to go back." I fumble around in my pocket for my phone, but it is now on the floor of the car, bouncing around like a kernel in a popcorn machine. "I'm going to call my parents. I think—"

"No, please don't!" Nana Rhea pleads with a glance over her shoulder to me. The tires squeal again.

"Keep your eyes on the road!" I beg.

She snaps her attention back to the road but continues pleading, "*Please* don't call your parents. Your mom will come and take me back!"

"And what's wrong with that? Seabreeze Palms seems like a nice place!"

Nana Rhea sighs as she pulls us onto a narrow side road. The car's side mirrors are inches away from scraping parked vehicles. I think we're about to crash, when suddenly, she slams the breaks so hard, we both jerk forward.

The seat belt goes taut against my chest, and I let out a little "oof!"

For a moment, all I can hear is my fast breathing and my heartbeat thumping in my ears.

Nana Rhea puts her arm on the back of the passenger seat and swivels to face me. "I'm not sure you'd really understand, dear, but watching you pack up my stuff and then seeing them bring it into my new rooms..." She trails off.

"Yeah?" I squeak, still catching my breath.

"It made me feel so nostalgic, you know?"

She must see from my expression that I do not know what she means, so she continues. "It made me realize I'm not quite ready to give some of those things up. I thought I was, but maybe I'm not."

"Okay, well, I'm sure you can keep all your things at Seabreeze Palms," I say. I glance over my shoulder to see if anyone is coming after us. I closed my eyes for only two seconds! How had I fallen asleep so quickly? We're definitely going to be in trouble if Mom and Dad come back with food and we're not there. And no doubt Arnold is worried about where I am.

"No, no." She shakes her head. "It's not the things. It's the memories. It's who I *was*." She leans back in the driver's seat and looks toward the roof of the car. "I'm going to miss that house—I'm going to miss that life.

I know I technically stopped acting before you were born, but I hadn't realized how much it still is a part of me and I just thought..." She trails off again.

I narrow my eyes at her. "Just thought what?"

She claps her hands together. "One last night. That's what I need. One last night doing all the things I used to do when I was still on the big screen. I want to dress up and dance and eat expensive food and make bad choices and—"

"Make bad choices?" My eyes widen. It's not that I want to make bad decisions, but the chance to make *any* of my own choices is very, *very* tempting.

Nana Rhea turns back in the seat to look at me. "Oh, you're right," she huffs. "I can't go gallivanting around the city with you in the back seat."

"I didn't say that!" I sputter. I have no idea what *gallivanting* means, but it sounds exciting.

The wheels start to turn in my head. There's an idea forming—a small idea growing bigger and bigger, having to do with joining Nana Rhea for the night and winning my friends back.

But could it work?

If I can convince Nana Rhea to let me do things my parents would never allow, I can send photos from the night to Sadia and Tamzin so they can see me doing cool activities. Then they'll see I'm still fun to hang out with, and they'll want me back at the sleepover! I've missed the daytime activities, but I might still be able to make it in time for dinner with them. This could be the perfect plan to make everything go back to normal!

Nana Rhea taps her chin, not paying attention to what I've said. "But I can't take you back to Seabreeze Palms either," she says to herself. "If they see me there, your parents will try to stop me from leaving. Your mom would hate the idea of me jaunting around Los Angeles. She'd worry about my *safety*. And she'll take back her keys!" Her eyes dart to the keys dangling in the ignition.

My mouth drops open. "How did you get those? I grabbed the keys from the valet!" I pat my hoodie pocket for the keys and hear them jingle.

She makes a face like I've missed something obvious. "I have a spare. Made it ages ago in case I ever needed to borrow the car."

I gasp. "Does my mom know that?"

"Why would she?"

"But—!"

"Maybe I'll drop you off at the front of Seabreeze Palms before they make me stop," she goes back to muttering to herself. "I can slow the car to a roll, and you can hop out."

"Take me with you!" I blurt.

Nana Rhea raises an eyebrow. "I don't think so," she scoffs.

Thinking fast, I do something that I've never ever, *ever* done before—I threaten my grandma.

I hold up my phone. "If you don't take me with you, I'll call my parents and tell them where we are. They'll come pick me up, convince you to go back to Seabreeze Palms, and take their car back."

Wow. Two lies and a threat? What has gotten into me today?

I gulp.

And what will happen if Mom and Dad find out? I've never even been grounded or anything! It's been bad enough just to get their disappointed looks!

Nana Rhea looks at me like I've sprouted a second head. She narrows her eyes. "What *exactly* are you saying, Audrey?"

I think quickly, piecing together my plan as I speak. "If you let me come with you *and* we spend the night doing a few things I choose to do, then I won't tell my parents where we are." My voice starts to shake at the end of my sentence—I'm losing this newfound confidence fast. Maybe I shouldn't have threatened Nana Rhea. Now I could be in trouble for that too.

Nana Rhea narrows her eyes just as the phone buzzes in my hand. I look down at the screen. It's Dad. What timing.

"It's my dad," I say, looking down at my phone screen. "They've probably come back with the food, and he's calling to ask where we are." I gulp and muster all my courage to add, "So, um, do we have a deal? Can I come with you?"

The phone continues to ring in my hand as Nana Rhea chews the inside of her cheek. I move to answer the call, thinking she's definitely going to say no.

"Okay, okay!" she blurts. "We have a deal!"

My jaw drops open. I can't believe she's actually said yes. "Really?"

"I guess," she sighs.

I'm too stunned to say anything else. For a moment, I just stare at her, waiting for her to take it all back.

"You better still answer that just so they don't think you're dead." She points to the still-ringing phone in my hand. "But don't tell them where we are."

I nod and swallow at the same time. Tentatively, I swipe my phone to answer the call.

"Dad?"

"Audrey! Where are you?! And where is Nana Rhea? We're in the sunroom with food, and we've been looking all over for you!"

I close my eyes and try not to think about how disappointed he is about to be. If I do, I know I won't be able to go off with Nana Rhea—I'll feel too guilty. No, I cannot let him get to me. Tonight is going to be my night. This is my *one* chance.

"I'm safe. I'm with Nana Rhea."

From the front seat, Nana Rhea beams at me.

"What?!" Dad bellows into my ear. "Audrey, you

need to come back. Where are you? Nana Rhea needs to be here. She can't—"

Dad continues to sputter protests, but I end the call. I know if I hear any more, I'll give in and tell him where we are. Part of me wants to do the right thing, and I know I should listen to that part, but another, much bigger part of me—the part that wants to have friends in seventh grade and make a few choices without being told no—seems to be in control right now.

"Well done," Nana Rhea commends with a nod.

My hands shake as I stuff my phone into my pocket.

Guilt hits me instantly.

Oh gosh. Did I just make a massive mistake? This night might cost me a lot of chores and grounded nights. Although without friends to hang out with, it won't matter that I'm grounded. I won't have anywhere to be!

Okay. I've made my first choice. I'm doing this.

I look up at Nana Rhea and smile for what feels like the first time in a while. I'm *happy*.

A wicked grin spreads across Nana Rhea's face as she turns back to the wheel.

"I think we'll both need an outfit change first, don't

you?" Without waiting to hear my reply, she turns the keys and revs the engine. The car whirs loudly before vibrating steadily beneath us. Nana Rhea reaches for the gear shift to put the vehicle in drive, and we take off down the road.

CHAPTER FIVE

NANA RHEA SLAMS on the gas so hard, I'm jolted back against my seat again.

"Wait!" I grab a handle on the car roof to help pull me forward. "Do you actually have your license? We almost lost a wheel back there!"

"But we *didn't*." Nana Rhea smirks. Then she spins the wheel, and we come dangerously close to oncoming traffic.

"Uh, I'm pretty sure you're supposed to at least try to stay in the lines!"

I hate to admit it, but maybe Mom was kind of right about her driving.

Nana Rhea rolls her eyes and pats the passenger seat next to her, one hand still gripping tight to the wheel. "Fine. Why don't you come sit up here, and you can tell me when we get too close to something? It's only my vision that's the problem—not my judgment. My judgment is still outstanding."

I decide not to mention that good vision feels like an important part of operating a car. If I give her sass, Nana Rhea might end our adventure before it's even started. Instead, I quickly unbuckle, climb over the center console into the front seat, and strap myself back in next to Nana Rhea. At least now that I'm in the passenger seat, I may be able to grab the wheel and change the car's direction if we start bouncing up on the curb.

A man ahead of us is about to step into the crosswalk, but when he sees the speed at which we're approaching, he jumps back on the sidewalk and shakes his fist after us.

I don't blame him. We really need to get off the road.

"Where should we get new clothes?" I ask, hoping we won't be in this car much longer. "Somewhere close?"

"The next street over has a great boutique." We zigzag through a red light. "Start to look for parking," Nana Rhea says. "Valet preferably. I never got the hang of parallel parking."

"There! A parking lot!" I point to a driveway on the right.

"With valet?"

"Maybe!" I really don't care if it has valet. I just want to get the heck out of this car.

Nana Rhea spins the wheel to make the turn into the lot, and I *swear*—at least for one second—the car has only two wheels on the ground. We fly over a speed bump into the parking area and head for the first empty spot. Again, Nana Rhea hits the brakes so hard, we both lurch forward against our seat belts.

She turns off the car and flips down the sun visor above her head to check her hair in the mirror. I, on the other hand, am still gripping the edges of my seat and trying to slow my heart rate.

I breathe in, I breathe out. I'm just happy to be alive.

"Coming?" Nana Rhea steps out of the car and flips her shawl over her shoulder casually, as if we weren't almost involved in about twelve crashes.

With trembling hands, I open my door and follow her out to the sidewalk. And wow, how good it feels to be on solid ground. We're on a main street with lots of shops and restaurants. People in trendy outfits strut past us, paying no mind to what looks like a normal outing of a grandmother and her granddaughter. They have no idea we've just ditched my parents at a luxury living community.

Nana Rhea leads us to the right, but after only a few steps, the smell of something delicious coming out of a restaurant makes my stomach gurgle. I'm still very hungry. It's way past lunchtime.

I point to the source of the smell—a fast-food burger shop. "Can we run in there really quick for something to eat? I haven't had anything since breakfast."

Nana Rhea looks to where I'm pointing and makes a face. "Not there."

I frown and continue after Nana Rhea, following

her lead. But after three steps, I remember our deal and stop walking.

Nana Rhea turns back to me. "Audrey?"

"In the car, you said we could do things *I* wanted to do." I point to the restaurant.

"You want a greasy burger?"

I nod.

"Really?"

I nod again.

She crosses her arms.

"That was our deal for me not calling my parents," I remind her in a small voice. "Do things I want to."

"Fine," Nana Rhea exhales.

Happily surprised she hadn't put up more of an argument, I pull open the burger shop door, and we march inside.

"Welcome to Goodtime Burgers," calls a teenage cashier behind the counter.

I order a cheeseburger with extra pickles, and Nana Rhea reluctantly orders a salad.

"That'll be eleven forty-five." The cashier punches buttons on a screen.

Nana Rhea reaches down for her purse. "Uh-oh," she says.

I shoot her a wary look. "What uh-oh?"

"I left my purse at Seabreeze Palms. I don't have my credit cards!"

"You don't have a way to pay, ma'am?" The young cashier eyes us warily.

Nana Rhea and I exchange a worried look. This could be a massive flaw in our plan. If we don't have any money, how will we be able to actually do anything tonight?

"Are you...are you Rhea Covington?!" asks an excited voice from behind us.

We turn to see a frazzled woman clutching four bags of food, a coffee, a binder, and a phone. She uses her knee to push one of the bags higher up in her arms.

Nana Rhea gives her a dazzling smile. "Yes, I am."

I sidestep behind my grandma. She's the one in the spotlight—not me. I don't *do* spotlight. I'm a deer in headlights, remember?

The woman's mouth drops open just as the binder slips out from her grasp and tumbles to the floor. She awkwardly reaches down to pick it up and stuff it back into her arms. Once she has it safely in her grasp, the woman looks back up at Nana Rhea. "I'm a huge fan. Huge! I've watched all your movies—ten times each, probably. I wish you were in even more films!"

"That's very kind. Thank you." Nana Rhea grins.

The woman looks nervous as she says, "I didn't mean to eavesdrop, but I heard you don't have your purse? I can buy your food for you!"

Nana Rhea beams at her. "You're too kind! But we don't want to be an imposition."

I give Nana Rhea a "what the heck?!" look. I have no idea why adults say stuff like this. We clearly need someone to pay for our food. Why doesn't she say yes? Mom and Dad do this when we go out to dinner with their friends. When the bill comes, they all argue about who is going to pay it, and I just sit there thinking, *If they offered to pay for it, let 'em pay for it!*

"Honestly, it would make my day!" The woman hikes up her bags in her arms again. "Then I could tell my friends I bought lunch for Rhea Covington and…" She looks at me expectantly.

"Her, uh, granddaughter," I answer softly.

"Wow! Her granddaughter! Well, I'd love to buy lunch for both of you."

"If you insist. That really is so sweet of you." Nana Rhea grins.

I let out a silent sigh of relief.

"What's your name?" Nana Rhea asks.

"April. I'm April." She giggles. "I can't believe Rhea Covington is asking for *my* name."

"Great to meet you, April. And thank you again."

After the woman hands the cashier her card, Nana Rhea picks up a pen from the counter and signs her name on a napkin in her big loopy handwriting.

"For you, dear." Nana Rhea hands the signed napkin to the woman, who looks at it as if it's a priceless artifact.

"Whoa!" She stares at the napkin. "Everyone on set is going to be so jealous."

"On set? Do you work on a film set?" Nana Rhea asks.

"Yeah! I'm a production assistant for the studio down the road."

April's phone rings and she shifts the items in her arms to look at it. She frowns at the number on the screen and moans. "I should get back to work. The producers will want their food and coffee. But it was an honor to meet you, and thank you for the signed napkin!"

"No, thank *you,*" Nana Rhea insists.

The woman gives us a wave before hustling out the door.

"That was lucky," I say as we head toward a table with our food.

Nana Rhea pulls another napkin out of our food bag and uses it to wipe off the plastic seat before sitting across from me in the booth.

I sit, unwrap my food, and take a huge bite of my burger. "So how are we going to get new outfits without any money?"

Nana Rhea curls her lip up at me. "Be polite. Don't talk with your mouth full, Audrey." She uses a plastic fork to stab a few pieces of lettuce.

"Sorry," I say, sighing.

I guess I should've known this night would have just as many rules as every other night. I should have added "no rules for Audrey" as part of my deal with Nana Rhea. All I thought to think of in exchange for not telling my parents where we are was "spend the night doing a few things *I* choose to do." Having no rules would definitely impress my friends.

I take a few more bites of my burger.

A thought forms in my head as I chew.

Although…doesn't doing what I want to do technically include me not wanting to have rules? Yeah, I could make that argument. In fact, I *will* make that argument.

"Actually, no," I say as I set my burger down, feeling a burst of courage.

Nana Rhea raises an eyebrow. "No what?"

"No rules for me tonight."

Nana Rhea crosses her arms. "First off, 'don't talk with your mouth full' isn't a rule. It's basic etiquette. And second, yes, there will be rules. You're eleven. I'm still in charge here."

"I don't mean, like, safety rules. I mean, like, you can't tell me what to eat, or how to act, or when to go to bed. That stuff. And I'm almost twelve."

Nana Rhea scoffs. "I wouldn't tell you what to eat or do. That's never been my style. You can decide those things for yourself."

I stare at her with a raised eyebrow. "Ten minutes ago, you didn't want me to come in for a burger, and you literally *just* told me what to do," I say matter-of-factly.

She puts a hand on her chest. "I didn't care if you ate a burger. *I* just don't care for them. And fine"—she nods—"I guess I am a bit of a stickler for etiquette and presentation. That's probably left over from my years dealing with the media. But other than that, I wouldn't comment on what you choose to do."

My eyes widen. "Seriously?"

"Yes, seriously. Where would be the fun in that?"

I sit back in my seat. If Nana Rhea was this cool while Mom was growing up, why does Mom get all strict with me? Seems like *she* must've had a pretty fun childhood.

"Well, thanks," I say to Nana Rhea with a smile.

She winks back.

Pleased with how this is all going, I take another big bite out of my burger and wipe my mouth with the back of my hand instead of using a napkin like my parents would probably want me to. Take *that,* Mom and Dad.

After a few more bites, I ask again, "Without money, how will we get new outfits? Or do anything else we want to do?"

Nana Rhea takes a few slow bites of her salad before answering. "Don't you worry. I know a place we can find new outfits." Nana Rhea gives me a mischievous smile.

"Uh, where?" I narrow my eyes at her. Old movie star or not, she's probably not going to get someone to pay for our clothes like we did with the food.

"Well, where I have in mind, they're not exactly for sale anyway."

"What does *that* mean?"

"We can just borrow them for the night."

"From where?"

Nana Rhea flashes her teeth at me in a wide grin. "The costume department at a studio lot, of course. That production assistant said there was one right down the road."

Even though I still have some chewed burger in my mouth, I grin widely. "Sounds like a plan," I say.

We finish our food and head back out to the street just as my phone starts ringing again. I pull it out of my pocket and frown at the screen.

"It's my dad again," I say with a grimace.

Nana Rhea rolls her eyes. "Maybe just answer to tell him one more time that you're safe with me, so he doesn't worry."

I'm pretty sure that no matter what I say, he's going to worry. But I listen to Nana Rhea and swipe to answer the call. After a calming breath, I say into the phone, "Dad, I told you—I'm safe with Nana Rhea. We—"

"Audrey? Stay where you are, all right? We've tracked your location based off your phone, and we're coming now to pick you up. We'll be there in a few minutes," Dad barks into the phone.

"You—wait—what?!" I sputter.

The line goes dead.

"They're on their way!" I say frantically to Nana Rhea.

"They're what? How?!"

"They have a location tracker on my phone. I totally forgot!"

"But we can't go back to Seabreeze Palms yet. All we've done is eat fast food! That's hardly the night I had in mind," Nana Rhea exclaims.

"I know!"

Nana Rhea taps her chin with a manicured fingernail and paces back and forth across the sidewalk. She snaps her fingers. "Get rid of your phone. We'll leave it in a trash bin and then they won't be able to find us."

I hug the phone to my chest. "No way! I'm not putting my phone in the trash. My parents let me have this one only because they thought it'd be useful in an emergency. They'll never let me have a new one if I toss it!" Also, even though I don't want to admit it to Nana Rhea, I need the phone to take photos of whatever we do so I can show them to my friends.

"Fine. Then leave it in the car. We'll lock it in the trunk so it'll be safe, and your parents will just track it to their car. We can leave the car anyway. We'll walk to the studio. April said it was down the street."

I make a face. That plan still means spending the night without my phone, but I can't think of a better solution. If I keep my phone with me, Mom and Dad will find us and take us back to Seabreeze Palms. But if I lock it in the car, I won't have it to take pictures. Plus, when my parents bought me this thing, they were pretty clear that I needed to keep it with me for emergencies. Leaving it feels…wrong.

"We don't have much time. Come on—let's hurry back to the car." Nana Rhea starts hustling away.

"But—" I look down at my phone. I need to make a choice. And quickly.

I glance up at Nana Rhea, who is looking over her shoulder at me with a pleading expression.

"Let's go!" she urges.

I gulp. What should I do?

With a deep sigh, I look back down at my phone. If I want to have this night, there really is only one option.

"I'll lock it in the car," I finally say with a grimace. I *do* want this night to continue, but I've never broken so many rules in such a short period of time.

"Good. Now come on!"

I hustle after Nana Rhea back to the car in the parking lot. She unlocks the trunk, lifts it up, and motions for me to drop my phone inside.

I hesitate. This is my last chance to call this whole thing off, go back with my parents, and accept whatever punishment I may get for *almost* ditching Mom and Dad. However, if I leave my phone here and go off with Nana Rhea, I might have some serious consequences waiting for me at home, but at least I'll also have a chance to prove to my friends I'm not as boring as they think. And I'll have the opportunity to experience things Mom and Dad would most definitely say no to.

Well, serious consequences, here I come.

I set the phone down, close the trunk, and wait as Nana Rhea relocks the car.

"Now we have to get away from here before your parents turn up. And fast," she says. "To the studio!"

Nana Rhea grabs my hand and speed-walks away from the parking lot.

There's a jittery feeling in my stomach as we hurry

away from the car, my phone, and my parents. At first, I think it's nerves, or maybe even guilt, but as I feel myself start to smile, I realize the jitters are something entirely different.

It's excitement.

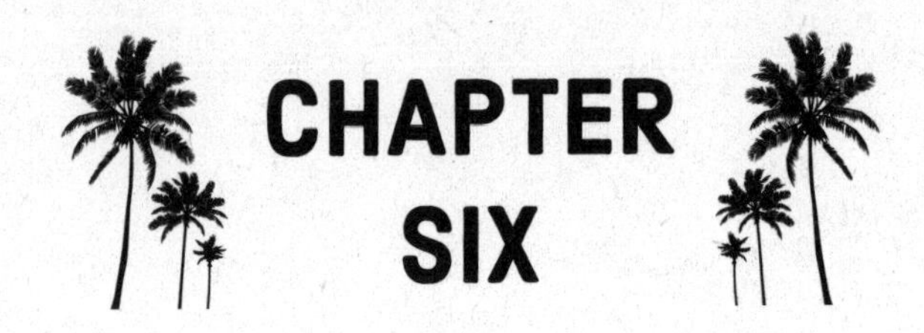

CHAPTER SIX

THE TALL, GOLDEN studio gate of Everest Pictures looms large ahead of us as Nana Rhea and I hustle down the sidewalk. Huge billboards hang over the street, advertising Everest Pictures' upcoming movies, and two buff security guards patrol the main entrance. It's eye-catching but very intimidating.

Nana Rhea and I watch as someone drives a car up to the gate, waves a badge in front of a sensor, which opens the gate, and passes inside. When the gate closes behind the car with a loud *clang,* I instantly realize the flaw in our plan.

"How are we going to get in?" I ask Nana Rhea. "We don't have badges."

"Leave that to me," she says as she pats my arm.

I hope she comes up with plans better than she drives.

We cross the road over to the golden gates and march up to one of the security guards, who looks at us through narrowed eyes.

Nana Rhea gives him one of her dazzling, movie-star smiles. "Hello. I'm Rhea Covington."

The security guard crosses his arms. "Sorry, no tours today, lady. There's something confidential filming inside."

Confusion flashes over Nana Rhea's face, but she quickly recovers. "No, no, we're not here for a tour. I'm *Rhea Covington*." She gives him her big, self-assured smile again. "I just want to show my granddaughter around." Nana Rhea wraps an arm around my shoulders and tugs me close.

The security guard looks at us from top to bottom. "You know how many people try to get in here by impersonating a celebrity? I hear it every day. I can't let you in."

"But I'm not an impersonator!" Nana Rhea protests. "I've shot many films here. I was in—"

The security guard rolls his eyes and cuts her off. "*Surrre* you were."

Suddenly, someone on the other side of the gate calls to the security guard, "Hey, Bill? Can I get your hand with something?"

The security guard shouts back, "One second!" Then he turns his attention back to us. "Now, can you two please move along so I can do my job?"

"But—" Nana Rhea starts, but he's already walking away.

When he's out of hearing range, Nana Rhea leans in close to me and whispers, "We need to come up with a story. Something that sounds plausible that will get us inside."

I make a face. While I have lied a few times today, I don't exactly like it, and I'm never particularly good at it. And even though my lies have worked, somehow I doubt any story I come up with will be able to fool this security guard who is *specifically* trained to keep people out.

"I don't know," I say, making a face. "I'm not—"

"He's coming back! Think fast!" Nana Rhea sucks in a breath. "Wait, I've got it!"

But before I can even open my mouth again, Nana Rhea stands up tall.

"Didn't I tell you two to leave?" a gruff voice snaps.

I turn to see the security guard towering over us again.

"Actually, we're here to see April," Nana Rhea says with all the confidence in the world. The panic that was in her voice two seconds ago is completely gone. It's like she's a whole new person—someone who really is here to see April. Nana Rhea continues, "She's a production assistant here, and she told us to come by."

I look at her, stunned. How did she just think of that? It sounds so believable, like April really did ask us to come say hello.

The security guard looks back and forth between me and Nana Rhea. Then he slowly unhooks a walkie-talkie from his belt.

"What's April's last name?" he barks at us. "I'll check if she requested day passes for you two." He clicks a button on his walkie-talkie and says into it, "Yeah, hey, Mike? I've got two people out at the Highland Gate entrance saying they're here to see a production assistant named April..." He looks at Nana Rhea to supply her last name.

Nana Rhea grins. "Oh, well, it's..." She pauses to think up a name.

Thankfully, a voice speaks out of the walkie-talkie before she has to come up with one. "You mean April Pinshell? She's a production assistant in building twelve working on that western sequel," the voice says.

I try to not let the relief show on my face.

"Yes, exactly! April Pinshell!" Nana Rhea says with a snap.

The security guard narrows his eyes again. "You're here to see April Pinshell? You're sure?"

I follow Nana Rhea's lead and nod enthusiastically.

"Hmm," the security guard says, shifting his weight, still eyeing us. "You two wait here. I'm going to go check the system to see if she requested passes for you. And if not, well, I can't let you in."

He stalks off, leaving Nana Rhea and me standing by ourselves in front of the gate.

"How did you do that?" I ask incredulously.

Nana Rhea sweeps her hair away from her forehead. "Do what?"

"Come up with that story so fast and make it sound so real!"

"I was an actor!" Nana Rhea laughs. "I can make anything sound real. It's all about putting on a character. I can be anyone I want to be. Besides, it's not that far from the truth."

"But, Nana Rhea," I say in a hurried low whisper.

"Yes?" She examines her nails.

"What do we do now? There aren't going to be any passes for us. He's not going to let us inside!"

Her face drops, and she bites her lip. "Oh, right. I nearly believed my own embellishment!"

At that very moment, a sleek black car pulls up to the gate next to us. A ring-laden hand lazily reaches out the driver's window and flashes a badge to the gate sensor. The sensor beeps, making the gate slowly creak open to allow the car to drive onto the lot.

"That's our way in," Nana Rhea whispers.

Before I have the chance to ask her what she means, she grabs my arm and pulls me to the other side of the entrance, away from the gate sensor. As soon as the next car pulls up to the gate, Nana Rhea tugs me into a crouching position beside the passenger side of the car so the driver can't see us.

"After this car opens the gate, we can sneak in behind it. We just have to keep close to the car so the gate doesn't close before we're inside," she instructs me in a low voice.

My mouth drops open, and a little shiver goes through my body.

Sneak in? I've never snuck in anywhere. Sneaking inside feels a lot different from telling a few little lies. I know I wanted to break rules tonight, but we could get in some serious trouble for this! Like actual, real trouble. Would this be considered breaking and entering? Could this go on my permanent record? And what even is a permanent record?

My stomach drops as I picture my name written on some official-looking document in red ink and all capitals.

"But—!"

The car starts moving before I have the chance to finish my protest. Nana Rhea hustles after it, still hunched over. I don't have time to think this through!

Okay, but if I don't follow her, I'll be left outside the gate all by myself. And I don't think my parents would want me to be alone. Right? They would want me to stay with Nana Rhea.

I think?

Yes. They would.

Wait—I don't want to think about what my parents would want me to do. What do *I* want to do? That's the whole point of tonight!

I pick at my fingernail. The gate is about to start closing again. I can't keep standing here—I need to do something!

I finally make a decision and run after my grandma, staying low so I'm not seen in the rearview mirror of the car. When I catch up to Nana Rhea, she grasps my hand and pulls me along. We make it onto the lot right before the gate clangs closed behind us.

That was a close one.

Nana Rhea and I exchange wide smiles. We've officially made it inside Everest Pictures.

The car we tailed pulls into a nearby parking lot, oblivious to the intruders it has accidentally helped get inside.

"Come on," Nana Rhea beckons. "Let's get away from the gate before that guard comes back looking for us."

We scurry farther into the studio lot, hustling down a maze of brick pathways. We turn left, then right, then left again. It's not until we're out of sight of the entrance that I feel safe enough to look around and take in our surroundings. And—ohmygosh—it's better than I ever imagined.

Everywhere I look there is something exciting to see. On one path there's a restaurant and a busy coffee shop, then on the next path there is a gym, a small fire station, a salon, and even a tiny bank. The smells of fresh paint and sawdust waft through the air, and when we turn a corner, I see people building a new movie set. Golf carts race in every direction, and people carrying props, clothes, lighting equipment, and lots of other things all scurry along the paths. It's like a mini city within a city!

"Whoa," I say, craning my head to see everything.

Buildings that look like massive warehouses line the small pathways, each painted with a giant number on its side. Fog billows out of a building marked **STUDIO 14,** and as we walk by it, two people dressed like aliens come out and go into a trailer with the label **MAKEUP**.

Nana Rhea looks right at home. There's a new bounce in her step that I didn't see while we were touring Seabreeze Palms. I wonder how long it's been since she's walked around a studio lot.

I'm distracted from my thoughts when I see a woman carrying a huge boulder.

"Look!" I point at the woman. "How is she doing that? It must weigh a ton!"

"It's not a real boulder. It's made from plaster and then painted to look like that. It's movie magic," Nana Rhea explains.

"Cool."

"Come on! Let's go this way to see if we can find the costume department."

We weave through a couple of busier pathways until we spot a man wearing all black rolling a rack of sequined dresses out of one of the warehouses.

"I'm bringing them back to wardrobe right now," the man says into a walkie-talkie. "The director didn't like the sequined options. So picky."

I silently motion to Nana Rhea that we should follow him. She nods in agreement.

We keep our distance from the man as he continues to roll the rack of dresses down the path, around to the left, and into a building with an enormous sign reading **COSTUMES**.

"Bingo!" Nana Rhea grins.

We duck behind a tree as the man uses his side to push open the door before tugging the rack inside. Before the door swings shut, Nana Rhea hustles out from our cover and uses her foot to keep it from closing. She waves me over to join her.

I double-check no one is around before racing over to her. Nana Rhea brings her index finger to her lips in a *shhh* motion as we tiptoe into the building and hide behind a tall shelf of colorful shoes.

From somewhere inside, the man says into his walkie-talkie, "I'm grabbing red and purple dresses. Maybe those will be better options."

A voice squeaks out of the walkie-talkie in response, but I can't hear what it says.

"Yeah, yeah," the man moans. "I'm coming back right now." He grabs a few more dresses, places them on another rolling rack, then exits out the same door. Luckily, he doesn't notice Nana Rhea and me crouching behind the shelf.

The door swings closed behind him.

For a moment, Nana Rhea and I are motionless and quiet, making sure we're all alone. When we hear nothing but faint noises from outside the building, we come out from our hiding place behind the shoes and gasp.

Thousands of clothing racks fill the room. It looks as if every dress shop in Los Angeles combined to form one massive, multilevel showroom. I've never seen so many clothes.

Handwritten signs dangle on wires above each rack of clothes. They read things like *Western, 1950s, Holiday*, and *Medieval*.

"This is incredible," I say, wonderstruck.

"Isn't it?" Nana Rhea runs her hand along a rack labeled *Ballgowns*. "I used to spend loads of time in the various costume departments while I was on set. I wasn't really supposed to be inside them, but the outfits were always too gorgeous not to look at."

I meander over to a rack with clothes that look like they've been ripped to shreds. The sign above the torn items reads *Zombies*.

Something sparkly catches my eye, and I turn to see an entire wall of organized jewelry. There are diamond necklaces in every shape and size, bracelets with tiny stones, and rings with gemstones as big as golf balls. There's even a beaded headdress that looks like it'd be way too heavy to actually wear.

"Incredible," I say softly as I lift some ancient-looking dangly earrings off the wall and examine them. Over my shoulder I ask, "How old do you think these are?"

Nana Rhea joins me at my side and peers down at the earrings. "Not that old," she points to the side of one. "See? The plastic is peeling here at the bottom of the earring. They were probably made a couple of years ago."

"But they look *ancient*!" I stare at the earrings in wonder. I wish I could wear something like these, but I don't even have my ears pierced.

"More movie magic, Audrey." She rolls her eyes. "Hasn't your mom taught you anything about Hollywood? She was practically raised with it."

I put the earrings back on the wall and gaze out across the room. "Not really. She doesn't tell me anything."

Now that I think about it, why doesn't Mom talk about any of this stuff? It's so awesome. She never tells me stories about being a daughter of a famous actress. All I get are the snooze-worthy stories about Dad's driving. Mom must have some good stories, especially since Nana Rhea seems like she was a cool parent, so why doesn't she share them?

"Oh, I thought she'd tell you about it," Nana Rhea says, almost a little sad. She runs her hand down a beaded jacket.

Feeling like I've said something wrong, I hurry to

change the subject. "What type of outfits should we pick out?"

Nana Rhea grabs a feather boa and tosses it around her neck. "Something fabulous."

She doesn't have to tell me twice. I head to the section of clothes labeled *Luxury* and start looking through the options. I'm pushing a hanger down the rack when my hand skims over something soft and smooth. I stop pushing the hanger and pull out the smooth fabric. It's a floor-length blue silk dress. And it's amazing. But unfortunately, it looks like it's made for someone double my height, so I place it back on the rack. If only I'd hit my growth spurt by now.

"What do you think of this?" Nana Rhea asks.

I pivot away from the blue dress to see her striking a pose and holding a red velvet jumpsuit up to her body.

"I've never seen you wear anything like that!"

"But I used to." Nana Rhea winks. "Not sure why I ever stopped."

"You should definitely wear it."

She glances at the dresses I'm flipping through

and raises an eyebrow. "Are you sure you want to wear something from that rack?"

I shoot her a furrowed-brow look. "You said you weren't going to tell me what to do. No rules, remember?"

Nana Rhea folds the velvet jumpsuit over her arm. "I only meant that you're looking in a section way out of your size. Why don't you go look in the kid section? I'm sure there will still be lots of lovely outfits that you'll actually be able to walk in."

"Oh," I answer sheepishly. "Right."

I make my way through the racks of clothes until I find the section labeled *Preteen*. Immediately, a glittery gold outfit catches my attention. I pull it off the rack and hold it up.

And I love it.

It's an amazing spaghetti-strap dress with beaded fringe at the hem that looks like it will fall just below my knees.

"That's the dress," Nana Rhea says, confirming my thoughts.

I spin to face her and see she's already quickly changed into the velvet jumpsuit.

I furrow my brows. "How did you—?"

"There's a tiny changing area back there." She points to the corner of the warehouse. "Go try that dress on!"

I look back down at the dress. I *do* love it, but I don't usually wear clothes that make me stand out. Glitter draws attention. Me and attention don't mix.

"You don't like it?" Nana Rhea raises an eyebrow.

"No, I do! I just..." I'm not sure how to explain my feelings on the dress. Especially not to her, queen of the spotlight, who can be anyone and say anything. She doesn't know what it's like to need to blend in. Nana Rhea doesn't keep quiet and act easygoing just to make everything easier. *She* has all the confidence in the world—no matter how people react. And she never seems to care what Mom thinks. I bet when Nana Rhea gets Mom's scrunched-eyebrow look, it doesn't make her feel all guilty.

"Go try it on." Nana Rhea nudges me to the changing area.

But...

Maybe I should try it on—you know, just to see

what it looks like. I can take it off before we actually go anywhere.

Yeah, I can at least try it on.

I hug the dress to my chest and hustle in the direction Nana Rhea indicated. When I come out five minutes later with the dress on, Nana Rhea claps and I, caught up in the moment, strike a pose.

"I think we've found our outfits for the night," she says.

I bite my lip. Do I really want to wear this out where people can see? Her praise does makes me feel like a million bucks. But is it *me*?

Nana Rhea's words from earlier come back to me.

It's all about putting on a character.

I guess I could wear this attention-grabbing dress tonight—you know, just to see if I even like clothes like this. Maybe tonight *I* can try on a character. I'll be a ruling-breaking, glitter-wearing version of myself.

I like the sound of that.

"Where should we wear them?" I ask excitedly. If my friends saw me now, there's no way they could think this outfit was *boring*.

Nana Rhea opens her mouth to answer, but before she speaks, the warehouse door creaks open, and a woman rolling two racks of clothes struts into the room.

We instantly drop to our hands and knees so the woman won't be able to see us.

"The brown vests are fine," the woman says to someone. "I think they're in *Western*."

"We don't need dinner jackets?" a second person asks.

Uh-oh. This is bad. We're no longer alone in here.

Footsteps echo near the racks of formal clothes. If they come around to the next rack, they'll see us hiding. And if they see us hiding and wearing these clothes, they'll turn us over to the security guards!

We need to get as far away from them as possible. Now.

I nudge Nana Rhea and motion for us to crawl away from the footsteps getting closer and closer. She nods and starts to silently crawl her way along the rack. I follow closely behind her, making sure not to catch my dress on any of the rack wheels.

We're almost around to the next row of clothes when one of the women says, "Deb, is this your shirt? I just found it on the ground back there."

I cover my mouth with my hand. She's found my clothes!

"Nope, that's not mine," the woman named Deb answers. "It looks kid-sized. Have we had any child actors in here recently?"

"I don't think so. Only people who work in the wardrobe department are supposed to be in here. It's too tempting for people to want to come in and try on outfits."

Nana Rhea and I exchange a sheepish glance.

"Then do you think someone took these off the rack and forgot to hang them back up again?"

"Doubtful. I was in here an hour ago and cleaned everything up."

"Wait, look!" Deb exclaims. "There's a pile of clothes here too. Blue pants and a shawl."

There's a beat of silence.

Finally, the first woman replies, "I think there's someone in here with us."

"What?" Deb sounds alarmed.

"Search the room."

Panic washes over me. Still on our hands and knees, Nana Rhea and I continue to scurry through the racks of clothes. But we don't have a lot of options of places to hide. Fast footsteps echo off the walls, making it hard to tell where in the room the women are searching.

It doesn't take long to figure out where they are.

"You two! Stop right there!!" one of them calls from behind us.

I look over my shoulder to see a woman in overalls pointing at us and frowning.

"You found someone?" Deb calls from across the room.

"Over here!" the woman in overalls shouts.

Nana Rhea and I scramble to our feet. My mouth goes dry, and I can tell by the look on Nana Rhea's face that she's not sure what to say or what to do.

This is bad. This is really bad.

"What are you doing in here?" the overalled woman snaps at us.

"We—uh—we—" I stammer. Apparently, this version of myself still isn't great at quickly coming up with fake stories.

"Huh?" The overalled woman doesn't look impressed. "Whoever you are, you're trespassing. And are you"—she eyes our outfits in disbelief—"wearing studio clothing?!"

Nana Rhea and I don't answer. I think it's pretty obvious we're wearing studio clothing. We're in sequins and velvet. Besides, if the fabrics weren't immediately obvious, I'm sure our guilty expressions give it away.

"Deb, call security!" she snaps.

"On it!"

There's a commotion as Deb fumbles to grab a walkie-talkie out of her pocket and trips over one of the rack wheels.

Nana Rhea leans close to my ear and says under her breath, "When I say *go,* we run for the door, okay?"

I don't even get a chance to process her words before the overalled woman reaches down to help her friend off the ground, momentarily distracted, and Nana Rhea suddenly whispers, "Go!" She pulls my hand as we bolt toward the door.

"No! Stop!" The overalled woman tries to grab my arm, but I just narrowly pull it out of her reach. "Stop!" she shouts again.

But we don't stop. We fly out the door and back out on the narrow pathway. As soon as we burst outside, we get strange looks from people walking by the building, and a golf cart has to slam on its brakes to keep from hitting us.

"Hey!" the driver shouts. "Watch where you're going!"

"Sorry!" I call back. My head whips from side to side, looking for the best way to escape.

"They're trespassers!" the overalled woman calls from behind us. I quickly turn to see her running out of the costume department door. "Don't let them get away!"

In the brief moment it takes for everyone watching to understand what's going on, Nana Rhea and I have already run out of anyone's reach. To keep from tripping, I have to hold my dress above my knees.

We head to the left, then right, then left again.

"Slow down," Nana Rhea pants. "I'm not as fast as you."

But we can't slow down. If we slow down, we'll be caught.

We speed around a corner and come face-to-face with the security guard from the gate.

"You two!" he shouts. "Stop running—you're cornered!"

We skid to a stop, and I let out a whimper. Behind us, loud voices are getting closer and closer. They're shouting things like, "They went this way!" and "Stolen clothes!"

We can't run forward, but we can't go back.

This is it. We've been caught. There's no way Nana Rhea and I can run past this security guard. And even if there *were* somewhere we could go, I'm not sure we'd have the energy. I can still hear Nana Rhea struggling to catch her breath beside me.

I'm about to hang my head and apologize for everything, when—out of the corner of my eye—I spot a golf cart parked just to the right of us. Its keys are still dangling in the ignition, as if someone's left the cart only for a second and plans to come right back.

The security guard takes a step forward. "It's over. Stop running. You've got nowhere to go." He bends his knees and holds his arms out wide, like he plans to snatch us up and haul us off to studio jail.

If he catches us, my parents will come pick us up, drag us back to Seabreeze Palms, and end our rules-free night together. I can't let that happen.

Without fully thinking through my plan, I grab Nana Rhea's hand and lunge for the golf cart, dragging her with me.

"Hey!" The security guard lumbers toward us, but I'm already climbing into the driver's seat and twisting the keys in the ignition.

The golf cart shakes to life.

"Go!" Nana Rhea says as she slides into the passenger seat.

I stomp on the gas, silently praying that golf cart driving is easy to pick up. The only other thing I've ever driven is a bumper car at the fair. And I was trying to hit things while steering that.

There's a squeal as the golf cart takes off down the narrow pathway.

Someone behind us shouts, "They've stolen a cart! Lock the main gate!"

Oh God. *Stolen*. There's that terrible word again. First the clothes, now this.

I want to yell over my shoulder back to them that we're only *borrowing* the cart, but I'm terrified that if I take my eyes off where we're going, I'll drive us right into the side of a building. I need to get us through the gate and back to the street before we're trapped in here.

I spin the wheel, and we skitter onto the next side path, weaving in and out of people hurrying to get out of our way. I'm not even sure if we're heading in the right direction. For all I know, I could be driving us back to the center of the studio.

"Look there!" Nana Rhea points ahead to where the massive gate is slowly closing.

I huff out a sigh of relief, happy to at least be on the correct path out. But the gate is still closing—there's only a small gap between them left. If we don't reach the barrier in the next ten seconds, we'll run straight into the metal bars!

"We can make it," Nana Rhea confidently declares. But even as she says it, she grabs the bottom of her seat to brace herself for impact.

Since I'm driving, I don't have any extra hands to hold something to keep me from flying into the small windshield if we collide. My only option is to get this golf cart through the gate.

I stomp down harder on the gas pedal.

We're not going to make it.

We're not going to make it.

We're not—

No—we *are* going to make it! There's still enough space to race through the gap in the closing gate.

But just before we're about to zoom out of the lot, a stunned voice from somewhere to our right says, "Rhea Covington?! What are you—?"

We don't have time to turn our heads to see who's speaking. Our golf cart zips out of the gate with only an inch on either side to spare. When we are finally free, Nana Rhea and I crane our heads back to see who called out to us.

And there, behind the now-closed gate, is April

from the burger store, watching us leave with wide eyes and a slack-jawed expression.

"Thanks again for lunch, April!" Nana Rhea shouts to her with a wave.

But I don't hear April's response as we continue down the sidewalk, driving farther and farther away from Everest Pictures.

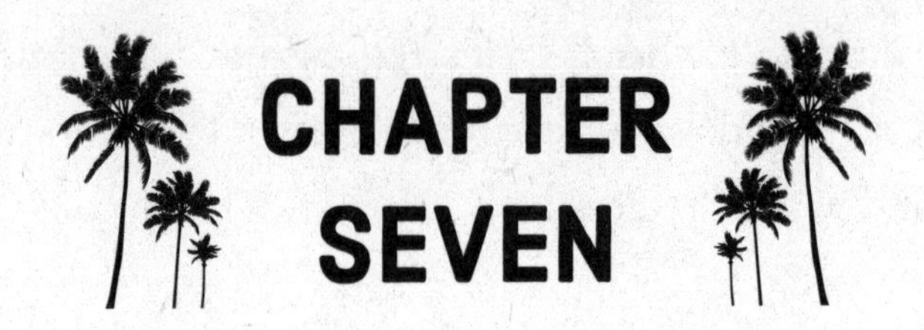

CHAPTER SEVEN

WE'RE ONLY THREE blocks away from the studio when I realize exactly what we've just done.

"We're going to be in so much trouble!" I sputter, still tightly gripping the wheel. "We stole these clothes and this cart and—"

Nana Rhea starts laughing. "It's okay, Audrey." She waves me off. "We'll return the outfits."

"It isn't funny. We trespassed!" I swerve the cart left to miss a lady and her small, fluffy dog.

"Of *course* it's funny. Did you see the look on the security guard's face?"

"Who *are* you?" I ask her. I want to turn my head to look at her, but I'm worried that if I take my eyes away from where I'm driving, I'll hit a lamppost.

"Sweetheart, I haven't felt more like myself in years. Besides, I thought you wanted to break rules."

"Well, yeah, I did." I shift in my seat. "But, like, small rules."

My parents are already going to ground me until the next century for ditching them and my phone. I don't need real crimes added to my list of offenses. I only need a little proof that I can do things my friends like to do—a few non-boring things—not lawbreaking things!

Then, as if responding to my thoughts, I see a shop that will give me *exactly* what I need.

I hit the brakes, and Nana Rhea and I both lurch forward.

"Are you done driving? Do you want me to take the wheel?" Nana Rhea asks with a raised eyebrow.

I try not to look horrified at her question as I answer, "Um, no. I want to go in there." I point to the shop we've stopped next to. The sign in its window reads **ROXIE'S PIERCING AND TATTOO PARLOR**. It looks exactly like the type of place this version of Audrey would like.

Nana Rhea follows my gaze and frowns. "Don't be ridiculous, Audrey. I'm a very understanding grandma, but tattoos at age eleven? Your parents would never speak to me again."

"I'm almost *twelve*. And I'm just going to get my ears pierced like my friends."

Newly pierced ears will be the perfect proof that I don't only do boring things. Once my friends see them, they'll have to invite me back into the group.

Nana Rhea lets out a relieved sigh and puts her hand to her heart. "*That* I'm okay with."

I grin.

"Although," she continues, "we still don't have any money."

My grin drops. Oh, right. That part.

"But let's ask them if they'd be willing to mail me a bill," Nana Rhea says as she steps out of the golf cart and marches toward the shop.

I scramble out of the cart after her, pleased that she's thought of a solution. As we step inside, a bell above the door chimes.

"Be right there!" someone calls from behind a curtain.

There's a whirring noise echoing in the shop that reminds me of the drills my dentist uses. It makes me queasy. They don't use drills to pierce your ears, do they?

Nana Rhea doesn't seem to mind the noise. She walks over to the counter and starts flipping through one of the binders atop it. I can see that its pages are filled with hundreds of black-and-white drawings. Nana Rhea nods approvingly at the ones she likes and sneers at the ones not to her taste. As she looks through the art, I sit on an old leather couch across from the counter and bite my nails.

When I stopped the golf cart, I thought this was a great idea, but now I'm not so sure. I think piercings hurt. I mean, duh, of course they hurt—it's a needle going through your skin! How could that not hurt?!

The whirring noise stops, and I pull my nails out of my mouth.

A tall woman with thick-rimmed glasses, bright-red hair, and tattooed arms walks out from behind the curtain and smiles at Nana Rhea and me.

"Hey, I'm Roxie. What can I do for you?" she says as she peels off her sanitary gloves and tosses them into a trash can beside the counter.

Before I can answer, a man with a white bandage wrapped around his arm walks out from behind Roxie.

"Thanks again, Rox." He tries to lift his arm to wave goodbye but winces in pain.

"Remember to put the ointment on. It'll help the tattoo heal faster," she instructs.

"Will do." The man nods with another wince. "See you soon!" The bell above the door chimes as he exits out to the sidewalk.

Roxie turns her attention back to me.

"Um, I'd like to get my ears pierced, please," I say, quieter than intended. It's hard to be brave when I can't stop thinking about that whirring noise and some big needle drilling into my ear. I don't want to leave this place wincing like that guy.

Roxie raises an eyebrow as she takes in my sequined outfit and windblown hair.

"Since I'm guessing you're not eighteen, I'll need written approval from a guardian to do that."

"That'd be me!" Nana Rhea closes the binder of drawings and comes over. "I'm her grandmother."

Roxie studies Nana Rhea in her red velvet jumpsuit. If Roxie recognizes her from any of her movies, she doesn't mention it.

"Ear piercing is thirty dollars total, including both ears and the earrings. Good?"

"Would it be possible for you to mail me a bill?" Nana Rhea asks, full of charm. She nods toward me. "It's her birthday, you see, and I promised I'd take her to get her ears pierced, but then, silly me, forgot my purse at home!" She bats her eyes.

Whoa. Nana Rhea really *is* good at this stuff. She almost makes *me* think what she's saying is true, and I obviously know when my birthday is, which is definitely not today! I can totally see why she won an Oscar for her acting now.

Roxie crosses her arms and looks back over to me. "I wouldn't normally do that"—she pauses as she continues to stare at me—"but since it's your birthday, I'll make an exception. I'll mail you the bill."

"Excellent!" Nana Rhea claps her hands together. "Thank you."

"Let me grab the paperwork for you to sign, then I can put holes in your granddaughter's ears," Roxie says.

I gulp.

Why did she have to say it like that? *Holes in my ears.* Now I'm positive she's about to bring out a huge drill.

Roxie walks behind the counter, grabs a few documents out from a drawer, and hands them to Nana Rhea to sign. Nana Rhea grabs a pen out of a mug that says ATTITUDE IS EVERYTHING! and elegantly writes her name and address on the document.

"Sweet," Roxie says, filing the papers away. "If you guys follow me to the back, I'll get you sorted."

Nana Rhea and I follow Roxie behind the curtain to where there are several comfy-looking recliner chairs lined up. Beside each chair are things that look like giant pens attached to long cords on metal trays. Roxie pats the seat of the closest chair.

"Have a seat here," she instructs.

I keep my eye on the pen thing as I sit. It does look suspiciously like something my dentist would use.

Roxie opens a drawer to the left of my chair and pulls out a wide plastic tray. She holds it out for me to see.

"Which earrings would you like?"

I peer into the tray and see about thirty stud-earring pairs, each pair wrapped in its own little baggie.

"Don't worry," she adds as I stare at the earrings. "All these options are stainless steel to reduce your chance of an allergic reaction. And the piercing needle we use is always properly sterilized after each use."

Allergic reaction? Sterilized?

I'm honestly unsure if her words are meant to make me feel better or worse. Before she'd said them, I hadn't even thought about possible allergic reactions or the cleanliness of the needles.

"That pair is nice." Nana Rhea points to the baggie with two blue stud earrings.

I nod but continue to stare at the earrings. All I can see are their tiny, pointy ends that are about to be jabbed into my ears.

Roxie puts a hand on my shoulder. "You okay? There's no pressure to do this if you don't want to."

I take a deep breath.

Do I actually want to do this? I guess I could always think of another way to get proof of my night for my friends. I don't have to go through with this. I get to make the choice.

Then I remember the ancient-looking, dangly earrings from inside the costume department. Now those would be awesome to wear. It's true that regular Audrey doesn't usually wear jewelry that stands out, but maybe tonight's version of Audrey does. I mean, I am already wearing a glittery dress. And maybe it would be nice to have the option to wear something like those one day. And if I got my ears pierced, I could have the chance to.

I sit up a bit straighter.

Yes, I do want to pierce my ears to show my friends, but I also want to pierce my ears for me. I want this.

"I want to," I say with confidence. "And I think I want gold earrings. They'll match my dress."

Roxie fishes out a pair of sparkling gold studs from the bottom of the tray. "What about these?"

"Perfect," I say.

Nana Rhea gives a nod of approval as Roxie puts away the tray and unwraps the gold earrings. Then she grabs antiseptic wipes and a purple marker before sitting in her chair and pulling on sanitary gloves.

"I'm going to clean your ears with these"—she holds up the wipes—"then I'll use this marker to dot where your piercings will be, okay?"

"Okay."

Roxie leans forward, wipes my ears, then makes two marks, one on each of my earlobes.

"Now..." Roxie caps the marker and sets it on the tray. She picks up a silver needle smaller than her pinky finger. "You're going to take a deep breath, count to three, and by the time you're done counting, your first ear will be pierced."

"Wait," I say, looking at the small needle in her hand. "That's it? No drills? No scary tools?"

Roxie smiles. "This is it! Just this needle tool. It's going to feel like I'm quickly poking your ear."

"Oh!" I let out a sigh of relief. "All right."

Nana Rhea takes my hand in hers and gives it a squeeze.

"Ready?" Roxie scoots closer. "On the count of three."

I close my eyes, take a deep breath, and start. "One, two—"

Before I get to three, there's a pinching sensation, and my earlobe goes hot. It doesn't exactly hurt, but it's not very comfortable either.

"Three," I say as I open my eyes.

"One ear down," Roxie cheerfully says.

My pierced ear is already returning to its normal temperature. I feel the slight extra weight of the earring, but that's it.

I give a triumphant smile to Nana Rhea, who grins back.

"Ready for the next one?" Roxie asks as she scoots her chair to my other side.

"Yes, I'm re—"

There's a loud thump from the front of the shop, and all three of us snap our heads in the direction of the sound.

"That's weird," mutters Roxie. "Let me go check what that was." She puts the needle away in a container, stands, and walks to the other side of the curtain. As soon as she's out of sight, I hear her mumble under her breath, "What in the..."

Nana Rhea and I exchange a confused look.

"Let's go see," says Nana Rhea.

I hop out of the chair and follow Nana Rhea back toward the front of the shop. When we push past the curtain, both of our mouths drop open.

An excited crowd of about twenty to thirty people has formed right outside Roxie's shop. Several of them have their foreheads pushed up against the glass, trying to get a better view inside. There's another thump as another person smooshes their face to the shop window and cups their hands around their eyes. When the crowd sees us, they begin to whoop and cheer. Roxie quickly locks the door before they come barging in.

"Uh-oh," Nana Rhea says.

"What's going on?" I ask, trying not to sound as worried as I suddenly feel. Something tells me Roxie's

Piercing and Tattoo Parlor doesn't normally have a crowd pushing up against the glass. I don't think these are people waiting for tattoos and piercings.

But before Nana Rhea or Roxie has the chance to answer, I notice the mob's T-shirts. Some of the shirts read I'M RHEA COVINGTON'S #1 FAN! and others say COVINGTON CLUB.

Oh no.

They're part of the Rhea Covington fan club.

"How did they find us?" I ask, stunned.

Nana Rhea is still staring wide-eyed out the shop windows. "News travels fast," she says. "I didn't even realize my fan club was still active. They probably heard what happened at Everest Pictures and came looking for us. I bet the golf cart parked outside gave us away."

"Rhea Covington! We love you! Keep making movies!" someone outside shouts, making the crowd cheer even louder.

Another loud thump from the storefront draws our attention. The crowd is getting bigger and rowdier. They begin to chant in unison, "*Rhea! Rhea! Rhea!*"

My pierced ear begins to throb on beat with their chants.

Nana Rhea takes a step back. "We should leave. If *they* know where we are—"

I gasp. "Then my parents probably do too!"

"Especially if someone in my fan club posted our location online. I bet your parents will be checking for stuff like that."

"Which means they could be headed here already!"

Nana Rhea shakes her head. "We won't be able to leave through the front door—not without them stopping me for a hundred pictures and autographs."

"Can't we just push through the crowd?"

"Not a crowd this size. The public always takes more than you give."

"I can help you ditch the mob," says Roxie.

We turn to face her. I'd almost forgotten she was still standing there.

"You can?" I ask.

"Definitely. I know who you are. And you're not the first celebrity to wander into my parlor. I didn't mention that I recognized you because most of the famous people who come in here just want to get their tattoos and be left alone. But I've got a few tricks to help out my clients when necessary."

"Thank you!" Nana Rhea claps.

Roxie motions for us to follow her back behind the curtain. "There's a back door, and I can help you get—wait." She pivots to face us. "What about your second ear?" Roxie points to my unpierced ear.

I stop walking and raise a hand to my bare lobe.

Yes, what *about* my second ear? As much as I don't want my left ear to throb as much as my right one does, I also don't want to have a lopsided piercing.

I'm just about to ask Roxie if she can pierce it super quick when I hear a familiar shout from someone outside in the crowd.

"Audrey?! Mom?! Are you in there?! You better come out this instant if you are!"

I gasp. "My parents are here!" I tug on Nana Rhea's arm. "Then there's no time to do my other ear. We have to go!"

"Your parents?" Roxie crosses her arms, looking

concerned. "Why are you trying to get away from your parents?"

"We, uh..." I gulp. "Well, you see, we..." I swallow again, trying to regain composure.

Again, Nana Rhea's words from earlier echo in my head. *I can be anyone I want to be.* Right now, I want to be someone who sounds confident.

I take a deep breath and say in a steady voice, "We're doing a scavenger-hunt-type thing for my birthday, and they're trying to find us!"

Roxie uncrosses her arms. "Got it. Fun! Follow me this way."

I grin. That worked nicely. It's just a *tiny* white lie. And it's not like it's hurting anyone.

She continues to lead us past the chairs, past another curtain, and into a tiny back room with a door. She pulls keys out from her back pocket, unlocks the door, and pushes it open to a narrow alley.

I'm surprised to see the sun has gone down since the last time we were outside. Now an orange haze hangs in the air, slowly being washed out by the darkening sky.

"This back street comes out to the main street, a few shops to the right. If you walk, the crowd will probably see you. But *this* will keep your parents from winning the scavenger hunt." Roxie fiddles with her keys as she walks toward something covered with a green tarp. She pulls back the tarp to reveal a black motorcycle.

In unison, Nana Rhea and I suck in a breath.

"I've got spare helmets and can give you a ride past the crowd." Roxie opens a compartment on the back of the bike, pulls out two helmets, and hands them out to us.

Nana Rhea takes hers, and I cautiously reach out for mine.

"It's been years since I've been on a motorcycle," says Nana Rhea, eyes twinkling with mischief. She tugs on the helmet and tightens it under her chin.

I hesitate. Out of every rule my parents have, I'm pretty sure "Don't go on a motorcycle" would be near the very top.

Roxie kicks her leg over the motorcycle and motions to the space behind her.

"Squish on," she tells us.

"It's okay, Audrey. You go in the middle," Nana Rhea directs me.

With quivering legs, I step closer to the motorcycle. A golf cart was one thing, but this? I've never been on anything like this before. Unless, of course, you count a regular beach cruiser bike—which I definitely do not.

"Rhea! Rhea! Rhea!" The shouts from the crowd bounce off the top of the parlor and into the alley.

My parents are in that crowd. Probably ready to ground me until I graduate high school. But I guess that's a worry for another time. For now, I just need to focus on tonight and getting away so I have more time to do more things with Nana Rhea.

Holding my dress down, I swing my leg over the seat directly behind Roxie and bring my arms around her middle to hold on. Nana Rhea quickly takes the spot behind me, creating an Audrey sandwich. Her hands reach past me and latch on to Roxie's hips.

"Hold on!" Roxie says as she kick-starts the engine.

It catches with a loud *rummmm!* and the bike instantly vibrates beneath us.

With one swift flick of Roxie's wrist, the motorcycle jolts out of the alley, leaving the parlor, the crowd, and my parents behind.

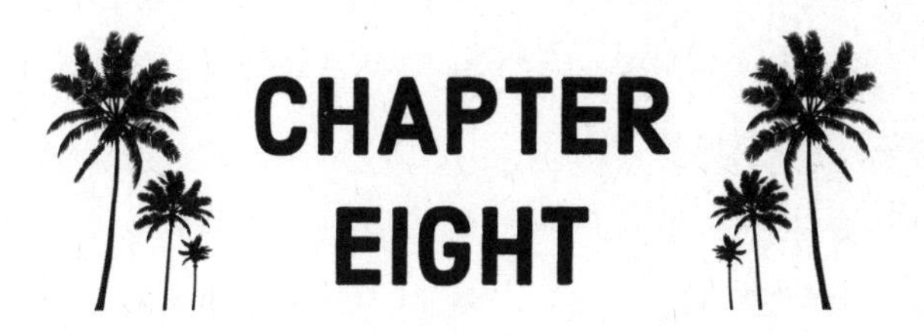

CHAPTER EIGHT

THE MOTORCYCLE'S ENGINE thunders down the street, and Roxie leans right and left, maneuvering us past cars and pedestrians. I have to close my eyes to keep from getting motion sick, but Nana Rhea laughs with glee behind me as if she's actually *enjoying* this.

We take a sharp turn, and I open one eye to peek where we are, but all I see are the blurs of trees and headlights. A sharp turn makes me lose my balance, and I gasp as I slip to the side. Luckily, Nana Rhea tightens her grip around my waist and hauls me back up onto the seat.

"Where should I drop you off?!" Roxie calls over her shoulder as we rumble through a green light.

"Do you know the Sunset Hotel?" Nana Rhea shouts into the wind.

Roxie nods and turns the bike left.

I squeeze my eyes shut again. I don't care where the Sunset Hotel is, or why Nana Rhea wants to go there—all I care about is getting off this thing in one piece.

The motorcycle whizzes through a few more turns before I start to feel our speed slow. I risk another quick peek just as Roxie kicks out her foot and stops the bike. I brace myself against Roxie's back as we both sway forward, then drop back down onto the seat with a thud. Slowly, I release my death grip from Roxie's middle and flex my fingers. They ache like I've just carried heavy grocery bags up ten flights of stairs. Ouch.

I have no desire, whatsoever, to travel by motorcycle again.

"The Sunset Hotel," Roxie says, motioning to our right.

Nana Rhea gets off the bike and tugs off her helmet. "It's just as I remember it," she says with awe.

After pulling off my helmet, I rub the feeling back into my hands and follow Nana Rhea's gaze to the gigantic building beside us. No wonder she wasn't impressed by Seabreeze Palms—this place is *way* fancier.

The Sunset Hotel has a grand marble entrance flanked with palm trees, spotlights, and flowering bushes. Its exterior is painted light pink and has intricate mosaic-tile designs running up its walls, making it look like something that would be in an advertisement for Italy or Spain or some other far-off place. Hotel staff stand by the main door in matching formal uniforms, ready to open it for guests.

"You two okay here?" Roxie asks, still sitting on her motorcycle.

"Yes! Thank you so much!" Nana Rhea takes Roxie's hand and gives it a big shake. "I'll keep an eye out for that bill in the mail."

"Half price since we only got to one ear." Roxie smiles. "Enjoy your night, okay?"

I return her smile despite the fact that my teeth feel like they are still rattling from the motorcycle engine. "Thank you for the piercing. And for the get-away ride."

She winks at me. "Keep an eye on your grandma. And win that birthday scavenger hunt!"

"We'll try! Thank you again for—" but before I can finish my sentence, Roxie takes off in a cloud of smoke. The noise of her bike fades away as she speeds down the road back toward her parlor.

I pivot to face Nana Rhea, who is still staring at the hotel in admiration.

"Why did you want to come here?" I ask, following her gaze to the building.

"I'm not sure," she sighs. "It just popped into my memory while we were on the motorcycle. I used to come here with various directors, writers, and costume designers. We'd all lounge by the pool and talk about our next movies. It was always a fun time."

There's a pool here? This news perks me up. I was

supposed to go swimming in Tamzin's pool today, after all. Although it may be a bit too late and chilly for a pool dip now. It's not fun to swim while your teeth are chattering. But maybe…

"If there's a pool, does that mean there's a hot tub too?" I ask.

Nana Rhea gives me a devious grin. "There is." She nods.

"Do you think we could go in?" I waggle my eyebrows.

"I think we should. The pool house will have suits we can borrow. If I remember correctly, the hotel is open only to guests, so act confident when we walk inside—like we're supposed to be there."

I bite my lower lip. "But, um, what do I say if I'm stopped or asked to show a room key?"

She waves me off. "Don't worry. We won't be stopped if we seem like we're guests."

I open my mouth to ask Nana Rhea how I'm supposed to act like a guest, but she's already striding toward the hotel entrance, so I have to hustle to keep up with her.

When we get to the front, two uniformed doormen say in unison, "Welcome to the Sunset Hotel!"

"Thank you," Nana Rhea says, flashing them her award-winning smile while stepping inside.

"Thanks," I mumble, hoping I haven't already given us away as non–hotel guests.

Like the exterior, the lobby of the hotel is painted a soft pink and is decorated with tiled murals. Large flower vases dot the room, making the air smell like lavender and eucalyptus, and there's a grand staircase on the far end of the lobby that probably leads to the rooms. In the corner of the lobby, there is the front desk, where two more uniformed staff members are looking down and typing away on their computers.

With her head held high, Nana Rhea strides past the front desk without stopping to speak to the receptionists. I cast my eyes down toward my feet and take quick steps to keep up with her. I feel very awkward. *Just* as we're about to make it past the front desk, one of the receptionists looks up and spots us.

"Excuse me, are you two looking for check-in?" the

receptionist asks. He has an over-gelled brown mustache that wobbles when he talks.

"Oh, hi!" Nana Rhea spins to face him and flashes her celebrity smile. "No, we're not looking for check-in." She moves to keep walking, but the mustache man looks between the two of us and frowns.

"Then would you mind confirming your room number with me? The hotel is actually open only to guests, and we have a private event happening tonight. I don't remember checking you in." He looks down at his computer, ready to type in our room number.

Uh-oh. We've been caught. Probably thanks to me. The receptionist must've noticed how out of place I look.

"I'm *Rhea Covington*."

I roll my eyes. Well, if *that's* what she was going to do, why didn't she say that in the first place? Would've been so much easier to lead with that.

"Sorry," he says, "I don't really pay attention to celebrity stuff. Are you a famous singer or something?"

Nana Rhea looks at me, then looks back at the receptionist.

Yikes. I guess the name-dropping didn't work.

"You know what?" She laughs. "Never mind. I think we've misremembered what hotel we're in. We must be staying next door. Apologies."

The receptionist smiles. "It's not a problem. Would you like me to help you locate where you're staying?"

She waves him off. "We'll manage. But thank you."

"Of course." He gives us a nod before looking back down at his computer as we glumly slink back out the front door and to the plant-lined sidewalk outside the hotel.

When we're out of earshot of the doormen, I sigh. "What now?"

Nana Rhea squints at the side of the hotel. "Maybe there's a side entrance we can go through to the pool area. If we go fast, maybe we won't be seen sneaking inside."

I make a face. Getting caught in the lobby was one thing, but what will happen if we're caught breaking into the hotel? Wasn't it enough to sneak into Everest Pictures?

Nana Rhea must see the hesitation in my expression, because she says, "Come on," and smiles. "Being a little naughty is all part of the fun!"

I bite my lip.

Am I having fun? I was nearly involved in a car accident, snatched by a studio guard, squished by a gigantic gate, and thrown off a motorcycle. Plus, I now have a lopsided ear piercing.

But, despite all that...yeah. I *am* having fun. I'm actually having the most fun since, well, ever. No one is telling me no—I'm getting to decide what I do. I can't believe I've never tried doing something like this before.

I give Nana Rhea my biggest smile. "Let's do it."

We creep around a row of bushes and toward the side of the hotel. When we get closer to the building, we hunch over so our heads aren't seen above the plants by the doormen. Through the bushes' leaves, we peer at the hotel, looking for an alternate entrance.

"See?" Nana Rhea points at an unmarked door behind a tree. "I bet that leads to the pool area without going past the lobby."

"Want to run to it on the count of three?" I suggest.

"Yes." She nods.

"One, two—"

"What are you guys doing?"

Nana Rhea and I jump in surprise and swivel around. Behind us stands a girl about my age with curly blond hair, wearing a fancy yellow dress. Her hands are behind her back, and she's leaning forward, trying to see what we're doing.

"Uh, no. We're not…um, doing anything," I say unconvincingly.

The girl rolls her eyes. "Please—you clearly are. You're being way too obvious about it too. I could hear you talking about sneaking inside from that window." She points to a second-floor window in the hotel. "I came out to join you. It looked fun."

Nana Rhea and I exchange a look.

"But if you were already inside, why would you need to sneak back in?" I ask.

She shrugs. "Seemed more exciting than what I was doing." The girl looks back and forth between us. "So where are you going?"

"We're just trying to get into the hot tub. That's all," Nana Rhea answers.

"Ooh, the hot tub," the girl says, nodding. "It's closed."

"Closed?" I ask.

"Yeah, someone accidentally got a hot dog jammed into the drain, so they had to close it for cleaning."

"A hot dog?" I raise an eyebrow. "How did that happen?"

The girls shrugs. "I honestly have no idea. I thought I had a good grip on it, but it slid right out of my bun."

I have to cover my mouth to keep from laughing.

Nana Rhea looks at me. "Ah, well, if the hot tub is closed here, maybe we should try another hotel."

"No, don't leave! You two seem like fun," the girl says. "I'll take you somewhere cool. And you won't even have to sneak in. Follow me!" She motions for us to follow her as she marches away from the bushes and back toward the front of the hotel.

Nana Rhea and I don't move.

"Come on!" the girl calls to us as she continues to stride away. "This way."

Nana Rhea and I both shrug at the same time before hurrying after the girl. When we catch up to her, she says, "I'm Eva, by the way. Eva Collins."

I have to take fast steps in order to keep up with Eva's pace.

"I'm Audrey, and this is my grandma, Nana Rhea—or, um, just Rhea, I guess, since she's not *your* nana."

"Audrey and Rhea. Got it." Eva nods. "You seem adventurous. I like that."

I try to hide my shocked expression. No one has ever called me *adventurous* before. I decide not to mention that. I want Eva to think I'm cool—anything to not be called *boring* again.

"Oh, thanks," I say, letting out a nervous chuckle. This is my problem with making new friends—I'm not exactly sure what else to say to her. Tamzin and Sadia usually do most of the talking. I try to think of something interesting as the girl leads us back toward the hotel lobby. What would tonight's version of Audrey say to Eva?

I'm distracted when I think of the person at the front desk. We'll probably get stopped again. Nana Rhea already told him we weren't staying at this hotel. He's going to wonder why we're coming back inside.

As we step past the uniformed doormen again, I hold my breath.

"Miss Collins," the receptionist says, sounding surprised to see her. "Is the party upstairs wrapping up?"

I tilt my head. Party? Is that where she's taking us?

Eva shrugs. "Nope! Just bringing in my two guests." She motions to us.

He looks over at us, definitely recognizing us as the people who just claimed to be staying somewhere else.

"These are your guests?" He raises a questioning eyebrow.

Eva nods. "Yup!"

The receptionist visibly swallows. "Your agent told us that your guests would not be able to attend today. We're not supposed to let anyone in who wasn't supposed to be here."

"Change of plans," Eva says coolly.

He swallows again, looking uncomfortable. It's clear he knows we're not supposed to be here, but for some reason, he doesn't want to tell Eva no. But why not? Who *is* she?

"O-okay. If you say so," he chokes out.

Eva nods. "Great, thanks!" She looks over her shoulder at Nana Rhea and me. "This way!" She marches toward the staircase.

The receptionist watches with a grimace as Nana Rhea and I hurry after her. We let her lead us up the stairs and to a pair of grand double doors on the second floor.

Eva motions to the doors and says, "It's a private party to celebrate one of Everest Pictures' new movies. They're not supposed to let anyone in who's not on the invite list. It's a good thing you have on those outfits—it'll make it easier for you guys to blend in." Then she pushes open the doors.

Nana Rhea and I gawk at the inside.

There's a mini red carpet, spotlights, and multiple cameras snapping photos. Adults in beautiful dresses and tailored suits laugh, dance, and drink cocktails out of very large glasses. However, the most eye-catching things in the entire room are the many posters and cardboard cutouts of Eva in an old-timey costume under the words **MOLLY'S WESTERN ADVENTURE**.

"Wait, this is a party for *your* movie," I say, slightly stunned. If she's an actress, I wonder why I don't recognize her, but then I see the film rating at the bottom of the poster—PG-13. No wonder I don't know who she is. I'm only allowed to see G-rated movies.

Eva nods. "Yup. It's my fourth one. Movie, that is—not party. I've been to loads of parties."

"Are those chocolate-covered strawberries?" asks Nana Rhea, looking into a corner of the room where there is a three-tiered chocolate fountain.

Eva follows Nana Rhea's gaze. "Mhmm," she says. "They have them at all these things. You can have some if you want. I've already had like six."

"I think I might just have to try a few," Nana Rhea says, her eyes twinkling. "You stay here, Audrey. I'll be right back."

As Nana Rhea hustles toward the food, a photographer snaps a photo of Eva.

"That was lovely, Ms. Collins!" they say before scurrying off.

"I don't think that picture will be very good," Eva pouts. "But," she exhales, "that's life as a celebrity.

People take photos all the time even if I don't want them to."

A wave of understanding hits me, and I have to keep myself from face-palming. Eva is an actress. Nana Rhea is *also* an actress.

"Did you recognize my grandma?" I ask. "Is that why you invited us in?"

Eva looks over to where Nana Rhea is loading strawberries onto a plate. She squints and furrows her eyebrows. "Um, should I recognize her?"

"Oh!" I answer quickly. "No—I just mean, some people do. I just thought that's why you brought us in. Because you recognized my nana."

"Nope!" Eva grins. "I've just been waiting *forever*"—she throws her hands up for emphasis—"for fun people to come to one of these things. When I saw you sneaking in, I thought you'd be good company! And kids my age never come to these things. It stinks." She frowns. "People think these parties are so exciting, but really it's super boring. I have to have the same conversation a million times, and my agent tells me I always have to be *professional*."

Eva talks in that fast way that always makes people seem like they have confidence—almost like her words are coming out faster than she's thinking them. People *have* to have confidence to talk like that because they have to trust they're about to say something interesting. It makes me like her.

Another photographer snaps a photo, flashing both Eva and me in bright lights.

"Thanks, Eva!" the photographer calls.

I have to rub my eyes to get rid of the light-induced spots.

"About what the receptionist said—I'm sorry your actual guests couldn't make it," I say when I can see properly again.

Eva sighs and looks down at her hands. "It's okay. They never do. My agent always puts them on the VIP list, but they're always too busy."

"Your friends?"

Eva looks at me with a raised eyebrow. "No, my parents."

"Ohhh," I say. "But if your parents aren't here, who watches you?"

"Watches me? Like as a babysitter? My agent, I guess. She's the one who drives me around."

Just then, Nana Rhea returns to my side with strawberries in hand. "You should try these, Audrey. They're delicious."

They do look good. And our late lunch feels like ages ago. On cue, my stomach gurgles loudly, making me feel like I need more than a couple of chocolate strawberries. I need a full meal.

"Eva, is there dinner food here?" I ask.

She nods. "Of course." She takes my hand and leads me to a long table in the back of the room that is covered in fancy-looking foods. There are whole glazed chickens, fish with the eyes still in, gigantic lobsters, and bowls of the most colorful veggies I've ever seen.

"You can eat whatever you want?" I ask incredulously. No wonder Nana Rhea liked being a movie star—she must've had meals like this all the time.

Eva nods. "Yeah! And there is always extra. My agent says the studio puts these parties on to butter up the members of the Academy before Oscar nominations. It's all politics, you know?" She tosses her hair.

I do *not* know what she's talking about, but Nana Rhea nods along as if Eva is making perfect sense.

"That's Hollywood," Nana Rhea says.

"That's Hollywood," Eva agrees. "Go ahead and fill up a plate. Then eat quickly so we can go explore the hotel together."

I march to the table and pile lots of different foods onto a fancy plate. Chicken, rice, potato-and-onion skewers, pastries—it all goes onto the stack. I stay far away from the fish with the eyeballs still in, though. It's odd to eat food that can stare at you. After I fill my plate as high as it can go without toppling, I dig in.

Nana Rhea scans the room as I eat. If I weren't so hungry, I'd probably be interested in people-watching too, but right now food wins.

As soon as I've taken my last bite of chicken, Eva tugs my hand.

"Come on!" she says. "Let's go do something fun."

Nana Rhea takes a step toward the crowd. "Oh my gosh! I see an old friend!" She waves to someone in the crowd before turning back to us. "I'm going to go say hi and mingle a bit, but you two have fun." She looks at me. "I'm trusting you not to go too far, Audrey. That's a safety rule. If I lose you, your mom will never let me see you again."

"I won't," I promise.

I let Eva lead me through the crowd.

"What should we do?" I ask.

"I don't know!" Eva shrugs with a smile, still weaving us through the fancy-dressed people. "It's just nice to hang out with someone who isn't asking me about my movies, you know? What do you normally do for fun?"

I bite my bottom lip as I think. What do I normally do for fun?

If I'd been asked that question yesterday, I probably would've answered, *I like hanging out with my friends!* And that's still true—except now that answer doesn't feel 100 percent correct. Or really, that answer doesn't seem *complete*. Because I can't remember the last time I hung out with my friends and had this much fun. It's been exciting just trying new things—even the scarier stuff—and I've liked being this new version of myself. In fact, this night has only made me want to experience more and more. And *that* part of the answer feels more...right.

"I guess I like trying new things," I say with a smile.

"Who doesn't?" She laughs. Then her eyes light up and she stops walking. "Hey, want to try something new right now? We could come up with a totally original prank!"

There's a pause as I mull the idea over in my head. Do I want to pull my very first prank? Yeah, I think that's something I'd definitely like to try. And like Nana Rhea said, being a little naughty is all part of the fun!

"Okay, let's do it," I say, a smile spreading across my face.

I look around the room in search of inspiration. Other than tons of elegantly dressed people, there isn't much to work with. My eyes scan over the section of the room with the chocolate strawberries. "We could do something with the chocolate fountain?" I suggest.

"Yes!" Eva claps.

Right when we change direction to make our way to the fountain, a woman with oversized curls and stiletto heels stands in our path.

"Ms. Collins! There you are," the woman says. "I'm Melly Leymonds from *We Are Live!*, and your agent said I could ask you a few questions about the movie. You don't mind, do you? Our subscribers are dying to know more."

Eva's face falls. "Now?"

"Yes, please!"

Eva looks at me, then back at Melly. She sighs and hunches forward. "Okay, I guess."

Melly whips a phone out from her pocket and taps a couple of buttons before pointing the camera at Eva. Eva instantly stands up a little straighter and gives the camera a wide, toothy grin. It almost seems like she's just become a new version of herself too.

"Hey, everyone watching from home!" Melly says. "We are live with Eva Collins, star of the new movie *Molly's Western Adventure*. Wave to your fans, Eva!

"So, Eva," Melly continues, "tell us all about your

experience shooting this movie. Isn't it so fun to be in the movie business? You're living every kid's dream!" Melly moves the phone closer to Eva.

"It's great to be the kid on set!" Eva answers enthusiastically, not seeming to mind the camera being shoved into her face. "The production team always puts out great snacks."

"Snacks!" Melly laughs. "You're adorable! Your parents must be so proud."

Eva gives the camera a thumbs-up. "I hope so!"

Melly leans closer to Eva, as if she's about to ask her a secret. "We've heard rumors there might be *Molly's Western Adventure, Part Two*. Is that true?"

"You know I can't tell you that!" Eva winks.

Melly waggles a finger. "You're not giving anything away, I see." She laughs again. "So tell us all about your friends! Is it hard for them not to be jealous of you and your celebrity lifestyle? What's your best friend's name?"

Suddenly, Eva's grin drops. Her face is turning red. "It's..." Eva awkwardly looks from Melly to me, then back to Melly. "It's, uh, well, it's...Audrey!" She finally says, her smile returning. "My best friend's name is Audrey."

My mouth drops. My name. Why would she say me? We barely even know each other!

Noticing Eva's gaze, Melly whirls the camera around to me. "Is that you? Are you Audrey? Oooh! Tell us all about being friends with a celebrity!"

Eva gives me an apologetic look, and I freeze, feeling like a deer in headlights again. I thought I was starting to feel more confident as this new version of Audrey, but who knows how many people could be watching Melly's livestream? All my regular shyness rushes back to me in one big wave. This is even worse than walking on stage at graduation. It's like the camera is magnifying everything about me for hundreds of people to privately laugh about or comment on!

"Excuuuse me, but are *you* Audrey?" Melly repeats. "The fans would love to know."

I don't reply. My silence seems louder than all the conversations in the room combined. Why am I not able to respond? It feels like there is glue coating the inside of my mouth, forcing it shut. After everything

I've done tonight, answering one simple question should be easy!

Thankfully, Eva steps between Melly's phone and me.

"We actually have to go, but thanks for the questions!" Eva says as she pulls me away from Melly's prying interview.

"Wait—but!" Melly sputters as Eva leads me back into the crowd.

"Sorry about that," Eva says once we're far enough away from the interviewer. "I shouldn't have said your name on camera." She picks at her thumbnail. "I kinda panicked, I guess. Since I'm always on set, I don't have a lot of friends my age. I didn't mean to put you on the spot or anything. I just couldn't think of my other friends' names." She looks sheepish.

Her honesty catches me off guard. If *I* were in her shoes, I'd be way too embarrassed to admit I didn't have any real friends. I'd keep my mouth shut like I always do when I'm too worried to say something in front of Tamzin and Sadia. I never want to risk my friendships.

Although…

For some reason I don't feel like that right now. Maybe it's because I don't know Eva as well as I know Tamzin and Sadia, so I don't feel like I'm risking an entire friendship by being honest. And I may not be a celebrity, and Eva may not know what it's like to have strict parents, but we might actually have something in common: We both don't exactly have friends right now. Weirdly, the thought makes me a little happy.

"It's okay," I tell her. Then I swallow my embarrassment and admit, "I don't have a lot of friends my age either. Or any right now, actually." I rub my arm, uncomfortable with the admission.

Surprisingly, Eva smiles. "Yes, you do." She links her arm through mine. "Anyway, for our original prank," she says, changing the subject, "what are you thinking?"

I grin at her. A friend.

She points to the chocolate fountain. "Still want to do something with that?"

I blink away the swell of emotion and focus on her question.

The chocolate fountain—right. What prank could

we do with it? I glance over to the food table and notice that there are two platters of brussels sprouts that have barely been touched.

"What if we dipped those brussels sprouts from the food table into the chocolate?" I say. "Then they will look like cake pops. People will have no idea there are veggies inside!"

Eva claps her hands together. "Yes! That's hilarious."

I beam at Eva's praise. The last time I suggested an activity to a friend, it was shot down as boring. This response is much better.

We hustle to the food table to fill up a plate of brussels sprouts and bring them over to the chocolate fountain. To keep people from seeing what we're up to, we crouch behind the fountain's table. There are toothpicks next to the chocolate that we use to stab the bottom of the brussels sprouts and then hold them under the dripping dessert. We giggle and share conspiratorial glances as we cover vegetable after vegetable in dessert sauce. It takes us a while to cover all of them, but when we do, we organize them on two platters to make them look appetizing.

Eva gives a wicked smile. "These look amazing. No one is going to be able to tell there are brussels sprouts inside."

"I can't wait to see someone's face when they bite into one of these," I say, chuckling, pleased with our work.

"Let's go offer one to my agent!"

"Okay!"

We stand, grab our platters of prank food, and turn to look for Eva's agent. But when I turn and see what's directly behind me, I nearly drop the platter.

There—standing with their hands on their hips—are Mom and Dad, staring down at me.

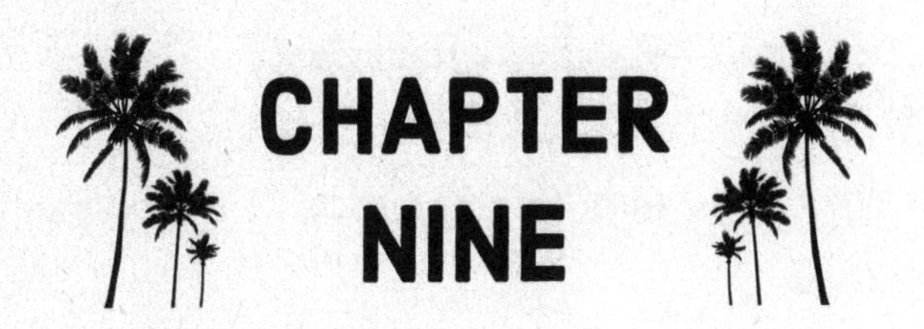

CHAPTER NINE

MY JAW DROPS open.

Mom's mouth is set into a deep frown, and Dad's eyebrows are lower than I've ever seen them before. They're still wearing their sweaty moving outfits and sour expressions, so they stand out against the clean and formal party guests.

How did they even get into this private party?!

I close my mouth and try to swallow. I should try to explain to them why we left and why I ditched my phone. I should grovel for forgiveness and promise not to run away again. I should say *something*.

But I can't. I clam up exactly like I did with Melly for *We Are Live!*

Eva holds out her platter of chocolate-covered brussels sprouts to my parents.

"Cake pop?" she asks tentatively.

"No, thank you," Dad says, still staring at me.

"What are you guys doing here?" I finally manage to sputter.

"What are *we* doing here?" Mom scoffs. "What are *you* doing here? Do you have any idea the night we've been through trying to find you?"

"We actually had to pay the man at the front desk just to come back here to look for you!" Dad huffs.

"I'm safe! I'm with Nana Rhea!" I say, craning my neck to look for her in the crowd. Well, at least I was with Nana Rhea.

Thankfully, she pops out of the crowd and takes my side.

"Exactly," Nana Rhea says. "She was with me."

Mom snaps a quick silencing glare at Nana Rhea before going back to frowning down at me. "I'm her *daughter*, Audrey. Don't you think I know the crazy trouble she can get into?" She shoots another look at Nana Rhea. "Honestly, what were you thinking? Thank goodness I had the idea that you might come to this hotel tonight. You were always here when *I* was a kid too."

"What's that supposed to mean, Kendra?" Nana Rhea shoots back.

We're starting to create a small scene. A few nearby party guests look over at us to see what's causing all the commotion. My neck shrinks into my shoulders.

"You know what it means." Mom swivels her attention back to me. "You're in big trouble, young lady."

"Yeah, I know," I huff as I set down my platter on a nearby table. "I'll be grounded for a long time."

"Grounded!" Mom barks out a laugh. "You think you'll just be grounded? Oh, no. More like grounded with no phone, no computer, no television time, and a new eight o'clock bedtime."

Nana Rhea crosses her arms. "That really doesn't seem fair, Kendra. Audrey wasn't—"

"Mom!" Mom barks. "Please do not argue with me right now."

Nana Rhea rolls her eyes. "Dear, if you hold an egg too tight, it cracks—it doesn't hatch. A little freedom would—"

"And what would you know about holding eggs too tight? You were off shooting movies for most of my childhood," Mom shoots back.

I recoil. I've never heard Mom talk like this. Nana Rhea doesn't deserve her anger. Nana Rhea has been helping me have more fun than Mom and Dad ever have!

"Those movies paid for your education!" Nana Rhea retorts.

"I would've benefited more from some actual quality time and guidance, rather than tuition for private school! Money isn't everything, *Mom*. Sometimes it *is* better to just do the sensible thing."

"I think that's enough for now," Dad says with an edge to his voice. "Everyone has had a very long day. Why don't we take Nana Rhea back to Seabreeze Palms and then head home with Audrey?"

"I don't want to go back yet," Nana Rhea sneers. "I'm an *adult*. I make my own choices."

Mom snarls, "You're coming with us!" at Nana Rhea, which starts them arguing again.

As they bicker, Eva leans closer to me and whispers into my ear, "Do you want to go home now?"

"No," I groan. "I was having fun."

"I was having fun too. I don't want them to make you leave."

"Me either," I grumble.

Eva straightens and gives me a wicked grin. "Then you should stay."

I give her a confused look. "How?"

She opens her mouth to say more, but Dad beckons me over to him.

"Come on," Dad says. "This night is over. We're all going home." He gives Nana Rhea a meaningful look before heading back toward the entrance.

Now that Mom and Nana Rhea have stopped arguing, the party around us has gone back to chatting and laughing. I send out a silent plea that one of them will stop my parents from taking me home.

But no one does.

Mom takes my hand and tugs me along. Apparently, I'm moving too slowly for her liking.

"This way," Mom huffs. "The car is parked in the front."

Mom, Dad, Nana Rhea, and I silently head toward the exit. I look back over my shoulder at Eva. What was she going to say? How does she expect me to stay after this? I want to stay, more than anything, but how?

I glance at Nana Rhea, who is begrudgingly following Mom toward the door. I guess she's not coming up with a way for us to get out of this. If I want to stay, it's up to me to figure out how. And fast. We're nearly to the double doors.

What would a *leading lady* do? A leading lady would take charge of the situation and get what she wants, no matter what attention it brings. That's what this version of Audrey should do.

Wait—that's it! I need to draw attention! But not just from anyone. I need to get the attention of—

"Security!" I holler.

Startled, my parents spin around to stare at me, confused.

"What are you...?" Dad starts.

"Security!" I shout again. I point at my parents. "Party crashers! They're party crashers! I bet they work for some entertainment blog and they're trying to find out secrets about the sequel!"

There's a collective gasp from the crowd.

Mom and Dad look around, stunned.

Dad puts his hands up and looks around the room. "No, we're not—" he tries to protest, but two tall people in security uniforms are already lumbering toward us to see what the commotion is all about.

"You four!" one of the security guards barks, pointing at Mom, Dad, Nana Rhea, and me. "Come with me."

"No, not them," Eva steps forward and motions to Nana Rhea and me. "They're my guests."

"You got it, Ms. Collins." The security guard nods. They turn their attention back on my parents. "Just you two then. We need to escort you off the property. Now."

Mom shakes her head. "There's been a miscommunication here. We're just picking up our daughter and my mother." She points at me and Nana Rhea. "I think my daughter called you so she wouldn't have to leave the party. Tell them the truth, Audrey," she urges.

I don't. And it sends a giddy shock through me.

The security guards cross their arms, not taking their eyes off Mom and Dad. "Are you on the party's guest list?"

"Um, well, no," Dad confesses. "But we were just—"

"Then you need to come with us." The second security guard takes another step closer to my parents. "This is an invite-only party. Very exclusive."

"Audrey! Tell them we're not party crashers!" Mom commands again.

I look between my parents, the security guards, Nana Rhea, and Eva. If I were going to tell the security guards the truth, I wouldn't have called them in the first place. There is no way I'm going home yet. Besides, how much worse can my punishment possibly get? I'm already grounded with no phone, no computer, no television, and an earlier bedtime. If that's what's waiting for me when I get home, then there's no way I'm giving up my freedom just yet. I want to see this night through to the end. Right now, I am the new adventurous, rule-breaking Audrey.

And this Audrey has more to do tonight.

My parents are still staring at me, waiting for me to speak up for them.

"Audrey!" Dad barks. "Tell the security guards we're here to pick you up!"

"Yes, tell them. *Now.*" Mom looks to Nana Rhea.

Nana Rhea looks at my expression, nods, crosses her arms, and stays silent.

It's not like anything bad is going to happen to my parents—they'll just be escorted off the property. And who am I to stand in the way of the guards trying to do their job?

"No more dawdling. Let's go," the second security guard huffs at my parents. "Out the front."

I didn't think my parents' expressions could look any madder, but as they reluctantly trail the security guards out of the dining room, I realize I was wrong. Very wrong. I've never seen them look so upset before.

I gulp. Yes, adventurous Audrey allowed my parents to be marched out of the party, but it'll be regular Audrey who will have to deal with the consequences later. Maybe that wasn't the best idea. Maybe I should've listened and gone home. Or maybe—

"We should get outta here before they figure out a way to get back in," Eva says as she sets down the platter and loops her arm through mine.

No. I did the right thing. *This* is what I want to be doing right now.

"Let's go out the side door and find a ride to the after-party," Eva says.

I raise an eyebrow. "After-party? There's a party *after* this party?"

Eva grins. "Yup!"

"I'm in," Nana Rhea says. "Can't even remember the last time I went to an after-party."

Luckily, once my parents have been escorted out of the room, the rest of the party guests seem to forget about my security-caused commotion. No one watches as Eva leads Nana Rhea and me through the crowd and out the double doors. As soon as the doors shut behind us, the noise of the party is quieted.

We race down the stairs and into the lobby. Once in the lobby, Eva doesn't march to the hotel front doors. Instead, she heads to the side of the room and slowly pushes open a hidden exit door. The three of us stick our heads out through the door gap and look outside.

Since night has now completely fallen, it takes my eyes a few moments to adjust to the dark. Instead of leading to the main sidewalk, this door opens to a side of the hotel where bushes and trees have been planted along a walkway probably used by staff members. If we take the pathway and go right, we'll end up at the back of the hotel. But if we take the pathway and go left, we'll end up back at the front of the hotel where we came in, and I'm positive Mom and Dad will be waiting for us there.

Eva points to the left. "The parking lot is at the front of the hotel. I have a limo that we can use to get to the after-party. Any sign of your parents?"

I squint down the path to where Nana Rhea and I pulled up on the motorcycle earlier. Through the trees and narrow path, I can't see much of anything.

"Nope," I say, shaking my head.

Nana Rhea says, "The security guards can only technically escort them off the hotel property. They don't patrol the public sidewalks. We'll have to move quickly so your parents won't spot us."

Eva says, "On the count of three, let's run to the parking lot and find a ride, okay?"

"Okay," Nana Rhea and I answer in unison.

Eva takes a deep breath. "One...two...three!"

On three, we burst from the side door and hustle down the pathway. Eva in the lead, then me, then Nana Rhea. Our feet thud against the concrete, and I have to duck under tree branches and sidestep large garbage bins. Soon, the path opens up to the front of the hotel, with its grand marble entrance flanked by palm trees, spotlights, and flowering bushes.

"There's the parking lot!" Eva pants over her shoulder as she points to the other side of the marble entrance.

"Audrey! Mom! Stop running, now!!" In the dark, it's hard to see the faces of the two people who dart out in our path and wave their arms. But I already know who they are.

Mom and Dad.

"Run! Go!" Eva calls again, laughing. Since she's not who my parents are looking for, she hustles past them without being stopped.

I, on the other hand, have to sidestep left to miss colliding with Dad. He quickly pivots, but I'm faster and duck under his arm. Mom lunges at me, trying to block me from running forward, but I spin out of her way.

"Audrey! This is ridiculous!" Dad shouts as I continue to race past my parents to the parking lot. "Stop running!"

I look over my shoulder to make sure Nana Rhea hasn't been stopped, and luckily, with my parents' attention on me, Nana Rhea has been able to easily hurry away from them.

However, if we don't quickly find Eva's limo in the parking lot, my security stunt will really have bought us only a couple extra minutes. Mom and Dad will be able to catch up with us again if we can't get away from this hotel. They've already started to run toward the parking lot after us.

"Keep going!" I hear Nana Rhea shout.

As soon as I enter the lot, I scan for moving cars.

"Do you see the limo?" Eva calls from just ahead of me.

I'm about to shout "no" back when suddenly, I'm blinded by headlights. I freeze. And *ohhh,* I guess the deer-in-headlights saying really *does* make sense.

"It's there!" Nana Rhea exclaims. I can feel her at my heels, panting as she keeps up with our pace.

"Get inside!" Eva directs.

"You better not get in that car, Audrey!" Dad calls from somewhere behind us.

I don't listen. The three of us race toward the headlights, throw open the limo's back door, and climb inside.

"Go! Go! Go!" Eva hollers at the driver before we've even had a chance to shut the door behind us.

The driver follows Eva's command, and the force

of the limo driving forward onto the street pushes me against the back of the seat. I watch out of the back window as my parents grow smaller and smaller.

It's only once I've had a chance to buckle myself in and turn around that I notice there's already someone in the limo—a man about my dad's age in a black tuxedo with slicked-back hair and bright-blue eyes, who regards us with a raised eyebrow.

"Oh, hi, Daniel," Eva says, still catching her breath as she leans back onto the leather seats. "Sorry, I thought this was my limo."

"It's not. I think your driver was waiting for you around the back," Daniel says, pointing back to the hotel.

Eva gives him a sheepish expression. "Well, since we're already inside, can we hitch a ride to the after-party with you? We're kinda in a hurry."

He gives her a suspicious glance. "Did your agent say it was okay for you to come to the after-party?"

She vigorously nods. "Yes, yes. Definitely. Yes."

"Good," Daniel says, nodding. "Then sure."

"Thanks!" Eva gives me another quick wink, which

makes me think her agent never said anything about going to an after-party.

Daniel clears his throat. "So, who are your friends?"

"Oh, right." Eva motions to us. "This is Audrey and Rhea Covington." Then she motions to Daniel. "And this is Daniel Davies. He plays my dad in *Molly's Western Adventure*."

"Wait." Daniel leans forward in his seat, eyes wide. "You're Rhea Covington? From *Beauty in the Wind*? That Rhea Covington?"

"I am," Nana Rhea says with a wide smile.

He claps his hands together. "You're a legend!"

"Thank you."

"I can't believe you stopped acting! You were so talented!" Daniel shakes his head. "I'd love to pick your brain about your work. Do you mind if I ask you a few questions?"

"Ask away," Nana Rhea says, widening her arms in a friendly motion.

Daniel sucks in an excited gasp and scoots forward.

I tune out Daniel and Nana Rhea's conversation and turn to Eva. In a low voice, I ask, "Won't your parents be mad when they find out you went to this after-party without telling your agent?"

She rolls her eyes. "Doubtful. In fact, they'll probably be happy I went if there are some big-name directors there. They'll probably think it could help my career."

I wish *my* parents would be happy if I ran off to a cool party.

"And your agent? Will she be mad?"

Eva looks out the window. "Yeah..." She pauses. "She will be." Her expression shifts to look a little hopeful. "And maybe my agent will call my parents and tell them I'm missing and then they'll come looking for me...like yours did."

I scoff. "Believe me, you do not want that."

Eva looks back at me with an expression that almost looks sad. But before I have the chance to ask her about it, she says, "Are your parents going to be really upset about what you did at the hotel?"

I widen my eyes and nod. "Definitely. I'll probably be in trouble for the rest of my life." I lean back in the seat. "Must be awesome to have parents who let you do what you want."

Eva opens her mouth like she's about to say something, then closes it. She glances out of the car window and her eyes light up. "There's the after-party house!"

I follow her gaze and peer out of the limo to see a ginormous gated house. The limo pulls to a stop, and we all climb out of the ride and straighten our outfits.

It's after-party time.

CHAPTER TEN

WHEN I THINK of a "home," the massive structure in front of me is not what I picture. The front of the house looks to be made entirely out of glass, metal, and concrete. And the landscaping is a mixture of gravel, grass, and tall hedges. It's all sharp angles and hard edges—nothing like the comfortable house I live in. Loud music and bright lights bounce out from the house and onto the street.

"It's the director's summer house," Daniel says after catching a glimpse of my open-mouthed expression.

He leans forward and whispers, "Kind of ugly, if you ask me."

I silently agree. When I own a house, I want it to be inviting, warm, and colorful.

Still, I can't deny that the lights and the sounds from inside make it seem like an exciting place to be. I've never been to a home like this before.

As the four of us walk toward the house, the music and the laughter from inside get louder. Its glass front door is propped open against a decorative planter, so we don't knock before stepping over the threshold and into the house. A long entryway opens up to a crowded main room, where people are dancing, singing, and swimming in a dark-blue-tiled indoor pool. The back doors are wide open, and I can see the faint outline of a moonlit gazebo in a yard that overlooks the city.

"Whoa," I say, catching sight of a glass indoor elevator and an aquarium with colorful fish that takes up an entire wall.

"*Whoa* is right," says Nana Rhea, who is to my right and also taking in the scene.

Daniel turns to her. "I must introduce you to some actors here. Everyone will be so keen to meet you."

Nana Rhea puts a delicate hand to her chest. "If you insist."

"I truly do. You're an acting icon!"

She beams. "I wouldn't say *that*."

I try not to laugh. I have heard Nana Rhea call herself exactly that.

"You are," Daniel encourages with a nod. "Everyone says they wish you did more films."

For the briefest moment, I think Nana Rhea looks uncomfortable. But then her smile pops back into place, and she says, "In that case, introduce away."

Daniel leads Nana Rhea, Eva, and me farther into the main room, and everywhere I look, there is something interesting to see. There's a woman in a leopard-print bathing suit doing back dives into the pool, there's a man in a yellow tuxedo doing the worm on a makeshift dance floor, there's someone holding a parrot and feeding it grapes, and there's even a magician doing card tricks.

Eva taps my shoulder to point out a gathering crowd, and we stop to watch as a stunt double demonstrates how to safely jump to the ground from the top of a staircase. We both cheer after he lands with a roll at the bottom of the stairs.

When the stunt double races into another room to show off another trick, I realize Eva and I have lost sight of Daniel and Nana Rhea. They've disappeared into the crowd. But before I crane my head to look for them, there's an unfamiliar voice from beside us.

"Eva! I didn't know you'd be here."

I turn to see a short woman with oversized glasses and pink cheeks grinning at Eva. She leans in and gives her a hug.

"Me? Miss an after-party? No way." Eva chuckles.

"You know, when *I* was a kid, my parents made me have a thing called a *bedtime.*" The woman laughs.

"Never heard of it." Eva shrugs.

I step forward and hold out my hand to her. "I'm Audrey." For once, I actually feel confident. And this feels like the best version of me.

The woman takes my hand and gives it a quick squeeze. "I'm Orsona, Eva's makeup artist. We've been working together since her first movie." She gives Eva a fond look before turning her attention back to me. "Are you a young actress too? Which makeup artist do you work with?"

"No, no. I'm not." I quickly put up my hands. "I go to school in Burbank."

"If you ever need a makeup artist, call me." Orsona grabs a business card out of her back pocket and hands it to me. "Orsona French. My number is at the bottom."

I look down at her card in my hand. It's light pink with gold edges and reads, "Makeup Artist to the STARS!"

"I've never worn makeup," I say, still looking down at the card.

"Not even just for dress-up?" Eva asks.

I shake my head.

Orsona holds up a large makeup kit. "Would you like to?"

I look up and grin. "Now?"

"Yeah! I'll give you some fun party makeup. I always carry my kit with me."

"Really?" A smile spreads across my face.

"Of course!" Orsona grins. "A friend of Eva's is a friend of mine. Let's go find a mirror!"

I scan the main room again for Nana Rhea, but she and Daniel are still nowhere to be seen. Daniel is probably introducing her to loads of people, so she probably won't even mind me getting my makeup done in another room for a few minutes. It is a no-rules night after all. And I'll only be gone for a few minutes.

"That would be great! Thank you," I say.

"My pleasure."

Eva and I follow Orsona across the crowded room and into a massive gold bathroom bigger than my bedroom. Orsona pats the countertop next to the sink.

"Sit up here."

I hop up on the counter with my back to the mirror as Eva puts the lid down on the toilet and takes a seat on it. Orsona sets her kit down on the counter next to me and begins to rifle through it.

"What color eyeshadow would you like?" Orsona asks.

"Um..." I bite my lip, thinking. I don't really know anything about makeup. I'm not even allowed to watch the cool beauty tutorials on YouTube—Mom and Dad only let me watch the educational channels, like the ones where scientists try to teach you how rocks are made.

"Well, what's your favorite color?" Eva asks, interrupting my thoughts.

"Blue," I answer quickly.

"Then do blue!" Eva says.

"But is blue a good eyeshadow color?"

"People look good in whatever they feel best in," Orsona declares. "If you like blue, let's do blue." She pulls out a skinny makeup brush and a round container of baby-blue shimmer power. "Can you please close your eyes?"

I shut my eyes, and a few seconds later I feel the stroke of the brush on my eyelids. The sensation makes me squeeze my eyes harder.

"Almost done," Orsona assures me softly. I feel a

few more brush swipes. "There. You can open them again."

I blink open my eyes.

"Ooh, that looks good." Eva gives me a thumbs-up.

Orsona pulls out a black tube from her kit and twists it open to reveal a tiny brush. "Now a little mascara. Can you look up toward the ceiling?"

I do as she says. I feel Orsona lean closer with the tube.

"This may tickle a bit," she admits. Orsona swipes the brush up my lashes, and I have to fight to urge to squeeze my eyes shut again. Thankfully, she quickly says, "Done!"

I glance back down from the ceiling and instantly feel the weight of the powder and the mascara on my lids. It almost feels like they are heavy with sleep. The sensation makes me blink a few more times. How are people not blinking all the time when they wear makeup? It's not exactly itchy, but I can definitely feel it.

Orsona takes a step back and assesses her work. "Very symmetrical," she says with a nod. "Except for..."

confession makes me feel slightly guilty about how my own parents are probably feeling.

The guilt makes me a bit ashamed. This night was just meant to be about making my own choices and winning my friends back by proving that I'm not boring. I was never *trying* to stress out my parents. I just needed a break from their rules—a break to find out what I like. I needed the chance to make my own choices.

But…maybe I shouldn't have left my phone in the car. And maybe I shouldn't have ditched them at Roxie's. Then ditched them *again* at the hotel. I just got so caught up in the moment. I've never felt this…free before, I guess. And now I'm hooked on this feeling.

Besides, Nana Rhea has been with me. So maybe it's not *that* big of a deal that I ran off.

Yet seeing the relief on Maureen's face makes me think otherwise. It feels like a really big deal. It feels like I've done something very, very wrong.

Eva's expression changes, and I can see her gulp. "Okay, sorry."

Maureen rises to her full height, and the softness disappears from her face. "Don't do it again, got it?" she snaps.

"I got it." Eva sighs.

"Good. Now unfortunately, we do really need to go, Eva. You have to be on set in the morning." Maureen gives me an apologetic glance. "Sorry to break up the fun. I hope we can find a time for you two to meet up again. Do you have an agent I should contact for your schedule?"

"Um, no. I don't have an agent," I say.

"I'll just get your number, Audrey," Eva says, pulling a sticker-covered phone from a hidden pocket in her yellow dress.

I recite my phone number as she punches it into her phone. "But I'm not sure when I'll have my phone back," I admit.

"That's okay," she grins. "I can wait."

I return the grin as Maureen ushers Eva toward the door.

"And Audrey?" Eva pauses for a moment in the doorway.

"Yeah?"

Eva says softly, "You're kinda lucky your mom and dad tracked you down at the hotel. I wish mine cared that much. You shouldn't wish to have parents like mine." She looks down at her feet.

My hands go clammy as I struggle for the right thing to say.

"Oh, I—" But I don't finish my sentence, because at that very moment a red-faced Nana Rhea appears in the hallway behind Eva and Maureen.

"Audrey Covington!" Nana Rhea snaps as she steps inside. "I've been looking everywhere in this house for you!"

I shrink back. Uh-oh. Now *that* sounds more like my parents.

"Nana Rhea, I was about to go searching for you," I say, my voice small and embarrassed.

Maureen looks from Nana Rhea to me before giving me one last nod of approval and nudging Eva out the door.

Eva gives me a tiny "good luck" wave before hurrying after her agent.

Now it's just me and Nana Rhea in the bathroom. And she's looking at me madder than I've ever seen her before.

"Why didn't you follow Daniel and me through the house?!" Nana Rhea huffs, hands on her hips.

I hurry to explain, "We did, but then we got distracted by a stunt double and—"

"You said you'd follow my safety rules. It's not safe to wander off by yourself! You can't do that!"

I cross my arms and hunch. I hate being scolded.

"You're starting to sound like my parents," I mumble, balling my hands into fists. Nana Rhea is beginning to remind me exactly why I needed this night. I wouldn't have *had* to run off with Nana Rhea if Mom and Dad hadn't given me such strict rules in the first place.

Eva doesn't know what she's talking about. I am not lucky that my parents tracked me down. She doesn't know all their rules and everything they keep me from doing. I shouldn't have to feel bad for wanting to win my friends back!

In fact, you know what? I won't! I will *not* feel

guilty. I don't care that Nana Rhea is upset. And I don't care that my parents are probably super worried about me. I've enjoyed tonight. And that's what matters.

"Maybe that's a good thing," Nana Rhea shoots back.

"I was totally fine!" I blurt.

"And how was I supposed to know that?"

I look down and grumble, "Maybe you could trust me."

"Trust you?" Nana Rhea looks taken aback. "Audrey, I *do* trust you. It's other people I don't trust. I know what Hollywood is like. Don't you think I—" She pauses, wipes a hand down her face, and continues, "If I didn't trust you, I would've never allowed you to come tonight. But rules are in place for more reasons than simply lack of trust."

I glare at her.

She glares at me.

"Come on, let's just…" Nana Rhea takes a deep breath. "Let's just go." She rubs her eyes.

"Where?" The question comes out a bit panicked. I am not ready to go back to Seabreeze Palms and have this all be over. I'm starting to really like this version of myself, and I don't want to lose her.

Nana Rhea gives me a long look, almost like she's thinking something over. Then she says with a sigh, "How about we calm down over some late-night hot dogs, okay? I know a spot around here that I used to go to while shooting my very first film."

There's a beat of silence before I finally answer.

"All right," I agree. I'm still pretty full from all the food at Eva's party, but it feels like Nana Rhea is giving me a peace offering with the suggestion, so I want to take it. Anything to make this night go back to how it was.

"It's close. We can walk."

"What about money?" I remind her.

"Already ahead of you." Nana Rhea reaches into a pocket of her jumpsuit and pulls out a twenty-dollar bill. "Borrowed it from Daniel. Figured we'd need it at some point tonight."

"Good thinking."

I hop off the counter, and we head through the after-party and back out the front door.

But as we walk along the dimly lit sidewalk, there's

still unspoken tension between us. The fun rule-breaking energy we started this night with has changed into something else. I can't exactly put my finger on it, but it's like we both can sense that this great night is almost over.

I do not want it to be over.

No. This is me now. And I'm going to make the most of the rest of this night.

I *have* to.

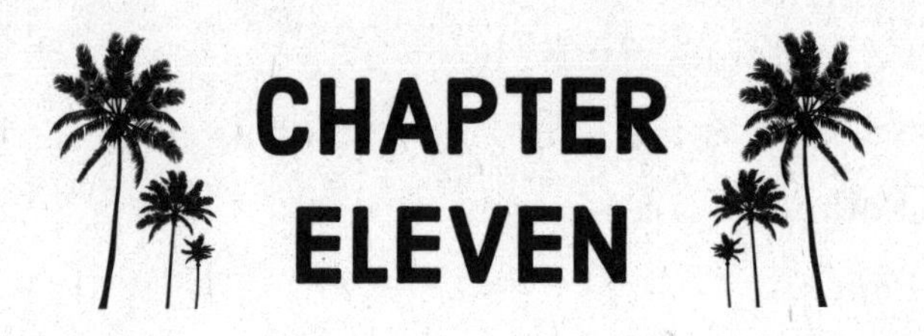

CHAPTER ELEVEN

NANA RHEA LEADS us along a quiet side street to a tiny restaurant that doesn't even have a sign hanging above its open door. If I didn't have her with me, I would've walked right past this place without knowing what it was.

"LA's best-kept secret," Nana Rhea says with a wink as we step through its entrance.

Inside, there are three red-topped tables, an old-fashioned TV mounted to a wall, and a large plastic menu stapled above a small counter. The entire restaurant is smaller than my bedroom. Heat from the back kitchen warms the space, giving it a cozy and comfortable feel.

"Welcome to Martin's!" a round-cheeked old man with oversized glasses says cheerfully as he walks out from the kitchen to stand behind the counter. "What can I getcha?"

I peer up at the menu. There are only two options: a hot dog or a hot dog with toppings.

"Two hot dogs with toppings, please," Nana Rhea quickly orders for the both of us.

I'd be annoyed that she chose for me if that wasn't the option I was going to pick for myself anyway.

"Excellent choices," the man says, grinning. "Give me about ten minutes to have your food out to you." He heads back into the kitchen.

"You'll love it," Nana Rhea assures me as we head toward the table farthest from the TV.

Once we sit down, I continue to look around the restaurant. This place doesn't exactly seem like somewhere the Nana Rhea I know would go. Didn't she say just earlier today that she didn't like food that came wrapped in greasy paper? And I don't think I've ever seen her eat messy food. Every time I've eaten a hot dog, half of the toppings end up in my lap.

Although maybe she used to eat messy food. Before tonight, it's not like I've ever seen her dodging security guards and riding motorcycles either. And she seemed to love doing *those* things. I *am* seeing a different side of my grandma tonight—maybe this is another place she's felt *nostalgic* for.

But...why now? She could've come here last week, or the week before, or whenever, really. If she likes this stuff so much, why doesn't she do it? I probably should have asked her this at the start of the night, but why did she wait until moving day to do all this stuff again?

I turn my head to the side, studying her. "Nana Rhea?"

"Hmm?" she answers, a bit distracted as she looks around the room.

"Why don't you come to places like this anymore?"

She turns her attention to me. "What do you mean?"

"In the car, when we first left Seabreeze Palms, you

said you missed your old life and that you were nostalgic for it. But then why did you stop coming to these places in the first place? Why come back tonight?"

"Oh, you know." She waves her hand dismissively. "I used to come to these spots while I was still acting, so it felt...odd to return once I stopped." She pauses, thinking. "But when we were packing up my clothes, I was reminded just how much I loved it—this life. And I don't usually care for this type of food *now,* but it just brings back such fun memories."

I nod. "You seem to like these places so much. Like the studios and the parties and stuff. You seem happy here."

"Yeah, well." She shrugs. "I was. I am."

"Then why did you leave them? And why quit acting? It seems like everyone wanted you to keep going."

Nana Rhea looks at me for a long moment. It's quiet except for the sizzling noises coming from somewhere in the kitchen.

"It's complicated," she finally says.

"How?"

Nana Rhea lets her shoulders sag a bit.

"Things don't always... turn out the way you think they will," she sighs.

I stare at her until she continues.

"You see"—she briefly closes her eyes and exhales—"after I had your mom and Gwen, I thought Hollywood would still want to cast me in leading-lady roles, like the ones I had before I got pregnant. And for a while, they did!" She forces a smile. But then it quickly fades. "Then, when your mom's father left, I wanted to prove to everyone that I still had life under control—that I could be both a single parent *and* a top-notch actress.

"So I went to even more auditions and parties, and I was getting parts, but I realized that as time went on and I got older, Hollywood no longer saw me as main-character material. I was being cast in roles that, personally, I thought were beneath me." She puts a hand on her chest. "I was an Oscar winner, for Pete's sake—not a background character." She chuckles.

"But," she sighs sadly, "the rules of Hollywood were changing, and people saw me as something different from how I saw myself. Suddenly, casting directors viewed me only as a mother of two teenagers. And I was that, yes, but I was *also* still the same leading lady as before."

I nod, encouraging her to continue.

"I didn't want Hollywood to make choices for me and tell me when I was done. I wanted to decide for myself! So I had two options," she says. "I could keep taking small parts and let the industry decide my legacy, or I could quit and define my career on my own terms. And that's what I did." She leans back in her chair. "With all the money I'd made from my older movies, it's not like I ever needed to work anyway," she scoffs.

"Oh." I frown. I'm not sure what answer I expected, but it wasn't that. "Well, what did my mom and Auntie Gwen say? Did they want you to keep acting?" I ask.

There's a beat of silence between us.

Nana Rhea looks away and bites her lip. "I'm not exactly sure what they thought. When I told your sixteen-year-old mom that I was quitting, she packed her bags and went off on a three-week road trip to who knows where."

My mouth drops open. "Oh my gosh. That sounds awesome! I can*not* picture my mom doing that."

"It was not awesome." Nana Rhea shoots me a look. "I had no idea where she'd gone."

"Yeah, but"—I raise an eyebrow—"I thought you didn't really care about that kind of stuff. You said it wasn't your style to tell people what to do."

Nana Rhea huffs out a breath and narrows her eyes at me. "I'm all for a little freedom, yes, but that was way too far."

"Yeah, but—"

"Who did your makeup?" Nana Rhea snaps, quickly changing the subject. Clearly, quitting acting and my mom are topics she no longer wants to talk about.

"Eva's makeup artist," I grump back. If she gets to be snappy, then I do too.

"I think you're a bit too young for makeup," she says.

I slump back in my seat and cross my arms. There she goes again, sounding like my parents. She's just crabby because I thought the road trip sounded fun. My makeup looks great. It—wait! I haven't actually seen my own makeup.

"Does this place have a bathroom?" I ask.

Nana Rhea thinks for a moment. "If I remember

correctly, there is one around that corner." She points to the left of the counter.

"I'll be right back." I stand from my chair to find the bathroom.

It has a heavy door that creaks when I nudge it with my shoulder and step inside. After locking the door behind me, I look into a small, yellow-tinted mirror and almost don't recognize myself.

My glittery gold outfit has dirt on the hem—probably road dust kicked up from the motorcycle—and a brown stain down the middle, which is most likely dropped chocolate, and blue shimmer powder around the neckline from Orsona's makeup. My one pierced ear does give my reflection a lopsided appearance, and the mascara makes my eyes look larger than normal. Plus, the lipstick makes my mouth look like I've eaten a whole bag of Flamin' Hot Cheetos.

I'm not sure what to make of the look. It feels like a stranger is staring back at me. A cooler, rule-breaking character that has confidence and awesome stories to tell. Is this what I wanted from tonight? Glitter, motorcycle dust, sweets, and makeup?

I wonder if this is what Mom's childhood was like while Nana Rhea was off at auditions and parties. If I were my mom, I'd talk about it all the time. How amazing would it be to tell my friends lots of awesome stories? And a three-week road trip without parents? That sounds incredible! Tamzin and Sadia would love it. It would be so cool to be this confident, rule-breaking version of myself all the time.

Well…

Sorta.

I kind of also want to feel a *teeny-tiny* bit more like myself. And this makeup isn't exactly *me*. I miss my old oversized hoodie. Since I left it at Everest Studios, will I ever get it back?

Using the back of my right hand, I wipe away some of the lipstick. I've decided I like the mascara, but I don't like having my lips this Cheeto-looking color. Besides, I don't want to get any of the lipstick on my hot dog and then end up accidentally eating it. I don't even know what lipstick is made out of. Yuck.

Once I've taken off the lipstick, I yank out a paper towel from a dispenser on the wall and run it under the faucet. Using the damp towel, I dab the different stains and marks on my dress, hoping to rub them clean. The plan was to return these outfits, after all. It wouldn't be good to give this dress back to the studio with this dirt all over it.

But unfortunately, all I end up doing with the damp towel is creating big wet sections on the fabric. It makes me look like I've lost a battle with a sprinkler. Plus, I can still see the blue shimmer powder around my neckline and a light-brown spot where the chocolate used to be.

Great.

With a defeated sigh, I toss the paper towel in the garbage, take one last look in the mirror, and march back out of the bathroom. When I turn the corner back into the main part of the restaurant, I see Nana Rhea standing back near the counter and talking to the round-cheeked man. I watch as she quietly thanks him and hands him back a phone.

That's odd. What was she doing with his phone? Did he recognize her and ask for a picture or something?

I walk up to her to ask right as the round-cheeked man goes back into the kitchen.

"Did he ask you for a photo?" I ask.

She jolts, clearly not realizing I'd stepped out of the bathroom. "What?"

"I saw you hand him back his phone."

"Oh!" She visibly swallows. "No. That's not it." She takes a deep breath. "Audrey, about tonight, I think—"

"Two orders of the late-night hot dogs!" the round-cheeked man calls as he quickly comes back out from the kitchen carrying two plates.

"Thank you," we say with smiles as we each grab a plate and take them back to our small table.

Relish slides down the back of my hands as I pick up the food and take my first bite. Nana Rhea was right—these are incredible.

We eat in silence. For some reason, Nana Rhea doesn't look me in the eye.

Suddenly, the sound of screeching tires outside pulls me from my thoughts, and I whip my head around to look out the open restaurant door. But what

I see makes me drop my hot dog onto the table, splattering ketchup down my front.

Just outside the restaurant, Mom and Dad's car is skidding to a stop. I watch as my parents fling open their car doors and begin to race toward the hot dog shop.

Panic spreads through me, and I whip my head around to face Nana Rhea.

"What are they doing here?!" I seethe.

She sets down her hot dog and frowns. "It's late. I think—"

"Did you..." I look up to the counter where the round-cheeked man was standing. "Did you call my parents on his phone?!"

She sighs. "Yes. I did. I think we've had our fun and—"

I quickly stand from the table, making my chair topple over behind me.

"Why?! Why would you call them? There are still more things we can do! They're going to end our night!" I fume.

Nana Rhea also stands. "That's not why I called

them. I called them because I realized it's the right thing to do." She reaches out as if she's about to rub my shoulder, so I take a quick step back. I don't want her to *soothe* me.

"No," I huff. "No, no, no!"

Nana Rhea looks apologetic. "I've had such an amazing day with you," she says. "But your parents—"

"Audrey!" Dad's voice calls from the restaurant doorway.

I snap my head back toward him. Mom comes up right behind Dad. They both stare at me like I'm a wild animal about to run. I wish I could run somewhere, but they're blocking the only exit. I have nowhere to go!

For a moment, no one says anything. The four of us just stand, staring at one another.

Just then, the round-cheeked man comes out from the kitchen and says, "How do you like your hot dogs?" But when he catches sight of our tense expressions, he spins on his heel and marches right back into the kitchen without another word.

After a few more silent seconds, Mom looks at Nana Rhea and snaps, "Thank you for *finally* calling us,

Mom. This night was so typical of you—no regard for anyone else."

"Don't say that to her!" I shout, but as soon as I say it, I want to take it back. I shouldn't be sticking up for Nana Rhea. *She's* the one who called them and ruined everything!

Nana Rhea puts up a hand. "It's fine, Audrey. She is right."

Mom continues, "Audrey would never normally do this. You've been a bad influence on her!"

Nana Rhea nods. "I know I should've called you sooner. I'm sorry."

"You're behaving just like you did for my entire childhood," Mom snaps. "Always running off to Hollywood."

I look back and forth between Mom and Nana Rhea. Uh-oh. This feels so much bigger than me.

"We can discuss all this in the car. Let's go," Dad says, motioning for me to come. "Night's over."

Tears start to well in my eyes. This wasn't how it was supposed to end. I know exactly what will happen as soon as I get in that car—I'll have even *more* rules than before. And I won't get to choose things for myself! I'll lose all this freedom.

No. No!

I just need a bit more rule-free time. More time to experience fun things. If I had a few more minutes, maybe I'd be able to think of a way to escape their rules and make sure there was no chance that anyone saw me as *boring* again. This is who I am now.

I need time. I need an exit. I need...

An idea springs to mind. I bet there's a second door out of this place that leads out to the street. Most restaurants have a back door that leads into their kitchen. I can probably buy myself some time if I run out that door!

Without a second thought, I back away from my parents, spin on my heel, and race past Nana Rhea toward the kitchen.

Behind me, I hear my parents sputter, "Stop! Wait!"

My shoes squeak as I slide around the counter and hustle to where the round-cheeked man went. I hear the sound of my parents starting to sprint across the room after me, so I pump my arms, trying to increase my speed. I have no real plan, no destination, and no money. All I know is that I'm not ready to go back to all those rules. I can't. There's no way I can let Mom and Dad decide what I do and who I am. Not anymore. I'm making my own choices now.

And yeah, okay, maybe the dirty-outfit and makeup-faced version of myself wasn't ideal, but it was definitely better than what I'll be allowed to be once this is all over. For once in my life I was starting to feel not as shy. I was starting to feel fun, and confident, and free. Everything that my friends—no, everything that *I* wanted to be.

I just need to figure out a way to not let that go.

I race around the counter and into the kitchen. There's a silver fridge, a long stovetop, and a sink, where the round-cheeked man is washing dishes. But the thing I care most about is the propped-open back door. I make a beeline for it right as the round-cheeked man looks up from the sink, sees me, and gasps.

"The kitchen's not safe for customers!" he says.

I don't stop. I run past him—focusing only on the open door. If I can make it out that door, then maybe

I can come up with a plan of what to do next. My feet thud against the tiled kitchen as I hustle to the door. I hear my parents hurry into the kitchen after me.

"Audrey!" they call.

"I said, the kitchen is not safe!" the round-cheeked man shouts again at all of us.

I push open the back door and sprint out onto the back street. If I had the time, I'd stop for a few seconds to let my eyes adjust to the dark, but since my parents are on my heels, I blink as I run to the right.

Luckily, lights from the street ahead come into focus. If I can make it there, I can get my bearings and sort out where to go next. Or even what to *do* next.

I push myself to run faster. Behind me, I hear my parents sprint out of the restaurant and begin to chase me down the sidewalk. They continue to shout my name as we run.

"Audrey!" they call, over and over. "Stop!"

I don't listen.

A tightness spreads through my chest. That sort of feeling you get when you're trying to hold down an oncoming sob.

Oh no.

Please don't let me be about to cry. I can't cry. Not now. Crying won't help me run faster!

I force the rising sob back down, making it sit in my throat like sticky food that's gone down the wrong pipe. It bubbles like it's not going to stay there for long.

Finally, I make it to the lit-up street. Unlike the road the small hot dog restaurant is on, this road is super busy. A crowd of people come out of a nearby theater, and I quickly weave in and out of them, trying to put as much space as I can between me and my parents.

"Stop running!" Mom calls from somewhere in the crowd behind me. They must've made it to the crowded street too.

My shoulder bumps a man dressed in a superhero costume, and he calls out, "Hey, watch it, kid!"

I keep going. I can't give up on this night—not yet. I will *not* stop running.

Because if I stop running...

The tightness squeezes my chest again, as if it already knows my next thought.

The sob in my throat starts to rise.

Because if I stop running, I don't know *who* I can be anymore.

My friendship with Tamzin and Sadia is over. I already know it is. I think I've known since they sent that text. But the longer this night goes on, the longer I can pretend I won't be starting junior high alone. And I can pretend that I can hold on to this version of me.

If I stop running, will everything go back to the way it was? Will I?

My right foot sticks to something on the ground, almost making me topple forward. I take a step back to unstick myself from whatever I've stepped on. I look down to see a big wad of blue gum stretched between the bottom of my shoe and the sidewalk.

No, no, no!

I lift my leg over and over, trying to unstick myself, but the gum string doesn't snap. And I have nothing to use to scrape the mess off my shoe.

The sob breaks free from my throat, and I scrunch my eyes, trying to stop the tears from rolling down my face. Through watery eyes, I look back down at my shoe, but something else catches my attention. The sidewalk I'm standing on isn't gray and cracked—it's pink. In fact, I'm not standing on regular sidewalk at all. I'm standing on a large tile with a pink star. In the center of the star, the name RHEA COVINGTON is prominently displayed over an old film-reel icon.

It's Nana Rhea's sidewalk star. The one she got after winning her Oscar. I must've run onto the Hollywood Walk of Fame! The star is a bit dirty from years of being walked over, but the grime can't cover its sparkle.

I let out another sob. *Why* did Nana Rhea have to call Mom and Dad? Like a punch to my gut, I remember what Eva said about my parents—that I was lucky that they cared so much.

Am I lucky? Right now, as I cry on the sidewalk with my shoe stuck in gum, I don't feel so lucky. I just feel tired. And sad.

I'm full-on crying now. My breath comes out in little hiccups, and I probably couldn't keep running even if I weren't stuck to the star. I guess if there was ever a sign that it was time to end the night, getting stuck on Nana Rhea's star is it. It's like the star itself is trying to tell me this night is over.

Fine, stupid star. *Fine.*

I'm still crying on the star when Mom and Dad finally burst out from the crowd, huff out relieved sighs, and pull me into a hug. I'm way too tired to shake them off, so we just stand there for a few moments with them embracing me as the people on the street walk around us.

"Come on, Audrey," Mom finally says, a slight shake to her voice. "It's time to go home."

I look up at my parents, tears still streaming down my face, and nod.

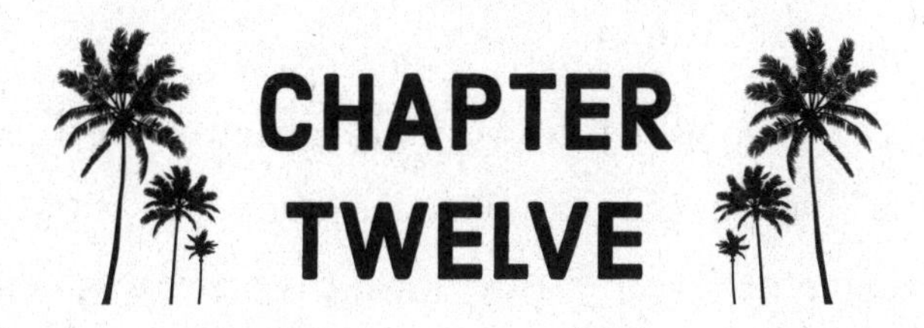

CHAPTER TWELVE

MY PARENTS AND I walk back to the hot dog shop, where Nana Rhea is waiting—two unfinished hot dogs with toppings still on the table in front of her. She stands when she sees us, gives a nod to the hot dog man, then follows us to the car.

Mom, Dad, Nana Rhea, and I drive to Seabreeze Palms in total silence. Nana Rhea sits in the back seat beside me, but I don't turn to look at her. She's the one who ended this night, after all. She doesn't deserve my attention right now. Instead, I let my head rest against the cold window as I watch the streetlights slowly go by. Every time there's a bump in the road, my forehead lightly smacks against the glass, but I'm too tired and sad to move.

Sigh.

It's not long before we pull in front of Seabreeze Palms. Even in the dark, it looks grand and fancy. I'm expecting people to hustle down the stairs to greet us, but since it's late, no one comes out to our car like they did before.

"Thank you for the ride," Nana Rhea says as she pops open her door. She pauses before stepping out and says to Mom, "Let's talk tomorrow, okay? We both have a lot to say, I think."

From the passenger seat, Mom looks over her shoulder and nods. "Yes, tomorrow. I'll call you." She sounds exhausted.

"I'll stay by my phone." Nana Rhea looks at me. She kisses the pads of her fingers before reaching out and touching them to my forehead. "Love you, Audrey. That was an incredible night."

I'm too upset to answer her.

Nana Rhea must understand I'm still angry, because she gives me a tight smile, blows me another kiss, then closes the door. I watch as she walks around the car and heads up the stairs. She gives the car a last look over her shoulder before marching into Seabreeze Palms.

Without another word, we take off back down the nearly empty street. Fog rolls out from behind palm trees that line the sidewalk, and the moon casts a strange glow over the houses. It makes the city seem kind of eerie—like the rest of the world is fast asleep. Or maybe I'm in a weird dreamland. Maybe this whole day has been a strange dream.

But the dream-spell is broken as soon as Dad pulls the car into our driveway. Back to reality. I march to my bedroom, not bothering to say anything more to my parents. They let me go without stopping me in the living room to give a lecture about everything I've done wrong today. I'm sure they're saving that talk for later.

Can't wait.

Not.

My packed sleepover bag is still in the corner of my bedroom. It feels like I packed it a long, long time ago—like I was a different person when I folded up my pajamas and stuffed them inside.

With a long sigh, I change out of the dirty dress, brush my teeth, and then climb into bed. I flip my body away from the door so that if my parents come up to check on me, they won't see my soon-to-be tear-soaked pillow.

I've never been so tired in my entire life, and it's not long before I fall into a deep sleep.

I wake up to Mom's voice echoing down the hall.

"It's early. I thought we were going to talk on the phone," she says flatly to someone.

I stretch my arms above my head and rub my eyes. They feel puffy and heavy. After blinking them open, I see sunlight streaming into my bedroom between the cracks of my window blinds.

"We were. But I decided I wanted to have this conversation face-to-face," Nana Rhea answers.

Her voice makes me sit up. Nana Rhea is here? At our house? What time is it?

I reach over to my nightstand for my phone before I remember I don't have my phone. It's probably still in the trunk of my parents' car. Ugh.

"Audrey is still asleep," Mom says.

I freeze when I hear my name. It feels like I've been caught eavesdropping.

"Good. Then just you and I can talk first," Nana Rhea replies.

I stay frozen in bed and try to make my breath as even as possible. They probably don't want me listening. Especially since Nana Rhea said it was *good* I was still asleep. I quietly lie back down and scoot my head along the pillow, closer to the door so I can hear them better.

Our couch squeaks, making me think they've sat down in the living room.

"I want to tell you how sorry I am about how I handled last night," Nana Rhea says.

"You should be," Mom snaps. "Do you have any idea how worried we were? It was the worst night of my life not knowing where my daughter was. And you stole our car!"

I cringe. I knew my parents would be upset, but I never thought it'd be the worst night for them.

"I know. Believe me, I know exactly how that feels. I should've kept you updated on our whereabouts."

"There shouldn't have been any '*whereabouts,*'" Mom scoffs. "You shouldn't have driven off with her in the first place."

Nana Rhea sighs. "I just thought she could do with a night of fun."

"That's what *you* needed. She's eleven!"

I want to grumble that I'm almost *twelve,* but I don't want them to know I can hear them talking about me.

"When you were eleven, you already had way more independence," Nana Rhea shoots back. "I let *you* decide who you wanted to be. I gave *you* freedom."

"Way too much freedom, Mom!" Mom says. There's a beat before Mom says in a softer voice, "I never talk about that time, because I made some bad decisions growing up, which I regret, since you didn't give me any structure. You were always off acting, and I felt like I had to parent myself. I'm *embarrassed* for Audrey to know about my childhood. Do you know how painful it was to remove that misspelled tattoo I got when I was a teen?"

I try not to gasp. I never knew Mom had a tattoo. It makes more sense now—why she never talks about growing up around Hollywood—I guess she doesn't want me to know about *her* bad decisions.

Nana Rhea starts. "I'm sorry, I—"

"When you told Gwen and me that you'd quit acting, I was ecstatic because I thought you'd quit to spend more time with us. But then I realized you didn't even quit for me and Gwen! You quit for your own personal reasons—to define your legacy—not to make sure your kids actually had a little guidance. That's why I took off when I was sixteen—because I was so upset!"

I hear Nana Rhea let out a little gasp. "I... I'm sorry. I didn't realize. I thought you wanted the freedom."

"Sometimes I did, Mom. But it's not up to the child to decide what they want."

There's another beat before Mom continues.

"I decide things for Audrey because I never want her to be in some of the situations *I* got myself into when I had no one setting rules for me. I want her to have a normal childhood. I don't want her to be unsafe or to grow up too fast."

The couch in the living room squeaks again. One of them must be shifting their weight.

"Listen," Nana Rhea begins, her voice soft and calm. "You're right. I see that now. And I did a lot of thinking after you dropped me home last night. I realize that I shouldn't have always been off to auditions and parties, and I should've had more structure for you and Gwen while you were growing up. I don't want Audrey to go off on her own solo road trip or anything like that either. And I get that you're strict with Audrey because I wasn't strict with you." She takes a deep breath. "But she *is* getting older, and if you don't allow her some freedom, she'll take it when you don't want her to—like last night."

Mom doesn't reply.

Nana Rhea continues, "I know I'm not really the best person to give out parenting advice, but it seems like if you let Audrey make some of her own choices now, then she won't grow up feeling like others are defining who she is and what she likes."

There's a long pause before Mom finally says, "I'm just trying to protect her." Her voice is so soft, I barely hear her.

"I know," Nana Rhea answers.

There's a sniffling noise, and I think...I think Mom has started crying! A rustling sound echoes into my room, which makes me guess that Nana Rhea is pulling Mom in for a hug.

"I was just so worried." Mom sniffs.

"And again, I really *am* sorry," Nana Rhea says after another long moment. "You, Audrey, and Gwen mean the world to me." The couch squeaks—probably from Nana Rhea standing back up. "So I hope you can forgive me. For everything. And I'll...I'll come back later when Audrey is up."

Another couch squeak. This time, I think Mom is standing up. "No, you don't have to leave," she says, voice hoarse. "Eric's in the kitchen making tea. Why don't you join us?"

"I'd love that." I can practically hear the smile on Nana Rhea's face.

As I hear their footsteps head toward the kitchen, Mom asks, "By the way, how did you even get over here?"

"Oh, Arnold from Seabreeze Palms drove me," Nana Rhea says.

"Mom, he's not your personal assistant!" she snaps, no longer sounding sniffly.

"What? He was happy to do it," she scoffs.

"Yeah, but..." Mom's voice grows fainter as she and Nana Rhea walk out of my hearing range.

I draw my blanket higher up my chin.

I knew after last night that my parents would be super mad, but I didn't realize Mom would cry about it too. Remembering the sound of her tearing up in the other room makes me feel guilty, embarrassed, and comforted all at the same time.

Eva's words from last night finally start to sink in. Her parents didn't have any rules for her, and she felt like they didn't care. But I know my parents care. I guess I am lucky to have parents like them, even if I still wish they had fewer rules. The thought makes me feel a teeny-tiny bit better. And even though she ended our night, Nana Rhea stood up for me. She thinks I should have more privileges too. So while I am still a little upset with her, some of my annoyance toward her eases in my chest.

I sigh. I guess I should go out there and talk to the three of them. I may as well get their lecturing over with and find out what my punishments will be. I'll probably be grounded until school starts again anyway. It's not like I have anything else to do. And now that I'm not Audrey from last night, I doubt Eva will want to spend much time with me either.

I pull back my covers and climb out of bed. A part of me wants to stay in my bedroom forever and not face the consequences of yesterday. But another part of me—maybe some leftover confidence from last night—knows that going out there is the right thing to do. I guess I do still have a bit of Audrey from last night left in me.

After a deep breath, I pull open my door and march to the kitchen in my pajamas. When I enter the room,

Mom, Dad, and Nana Rhea all look up from where they sit at our dining table. Mugs of tea and a few boxes of cereal are out in front of them.

"Good morning," I say, a little too flat to be cheerful. I may be a little less mad at my parents and Nana Rhea, but I'm not exactly in a good mood. I'm still going to be starting seventh grade with tons of rules, after all.

"Morning," Mom and Dad say in unison, a bit wary. They're probably expecting me to be a big grump.

"Hi, Audrey," Nana Rhea says.

Mom motions for me to sit in the empty chair beside her. I take another deep breath and slide into the chair.

Welp, here we go. Here come the punishments for all my rule breaking last night.

I'm about to open my mouth to quickly say sorry for ditching them, when Dad says, "We're glad you're safe, Audrey."

Mom nods. "Very glad. You really scared us."

"I didn't mean to," I say softly as I look down at my hands in my lap. "I just wanted to have a night where I wasn't always being told no. It's not fun being the only kid at school who's not allowed to do cool stuff."

Mom and Dad exchange a look. Nana Rhea focuses on the mug of tea in front of her.

"You shouldn't have run from us," Dad says.

"Three times," Mom adds.

"I know." I sigh.

"There will be consequences." Dad crosses his arms.

"I know." I sigh again.

"That being said," Mom says as she looks over to Nana Rhea, "Dad and I will have a chat about our rules and *possibly* expanding your privileges."

My eyes widen. "Really?"

"Don't get too excited. You're still going to be grounded for a long, long time *and* have extra chores this summer, *and* we're going to sign you up to do some community service. But"—she pauses—"we understand that you're almost in seventh grade and would like a bit more freedom."

"I just want to be able to try some new things. I don't always want to be told no."

Dad narrows his eyes. "What type of new things?"

"I want to be able to watch PG-13 movies," I blurt.

"You're not thirteen." Dad wags his finger.

"Okay, fine. A few PG-13 movies."

"None with violence," Mom declares.

"I'll take that. And I want to stay home without a babysitter."

"Not all day."

"A couple hours?"

"We'll think about it."

"And I want—"

"Why don't we just have breakfast together and go over everything else later, okay?" Dad says. "I don't think the day after you ran away with your grandmother is the best time for you to negotiate."

I blow a strand of hair out of my face. "Okay," I agree.

"Good." Mom stands from the table and walks over to the cabinet to grab another bowl. "At least you two didn't do anything *actually* illegal yesterday."

I glance over to Nana Rhea. She gives me a small smile that neither of my parents see. Mom and Dad don't really need to know about our trespassing or stealing. Those little details can stay between me and Nana Rhea.

I nod as I absentmindedly tuck some of my hair behind my ear.

"Audrey, what's that in your ear?" Dad asks warily.

My hand flies up to my earlobe and feels the gold earring I forgot was there.

I swallow. This talk had been going better than expected, but I doubt my parents will be happy to hear I pierced an ear without their permission.

"Like you said, you all can chat about everything later," Nana Rhea quickly interjects with a nervous chuckle. "Breakfast now?"

Dad looks like he might say something more about my pierced ear, but instead, he nods and pours some cereal into a bowl.

Whew. That was a close one. Nana Rhea to the rescue. Maybe my parents will forget about my one pierced ear and never bring it up again!

Unlikely. But a girl can dream.

Mom sets an empty bowl in front of me, and I pour myself some cereal. Thankfully, we move on from talking about yesterday when Nana Rhea switches the topic to how she plans to decorate her new place.

I try to focus on the conversation and not on the pressure in my midsection that squeezes when I think about my ending friendship with Tamzin and Sadia. What will next year at school be like? I can handle being grounded and doing extra chores—but can I handle making all-new friends at school next year? The Audrey from yesterday might have been able to, but can *I*?

"One last thing," Mom says, pulling me back into the conversation. She grabs something out of her back pocket and hands it to me.

It's my phone!

"You're letting me still have this?" I ask, surprised.

Mom looks over at Dad, then back to me. "We thought about it, and yes. We always want you to have a way to contact us, Audrey."

I look down at the phone and click it on, but the screen stays black. It must've run out of battery power while it was in the trunk of the car.

"And before you ask, yes. It still has location tracking. We aren't budging on that."

"Oh dear," Nana Rhea says as she abruptly stands from the table. "I've only just remembered Arnold is still waiting for me outside in his car. I should go."

"Mom!" Mom scolds.

"I'm sure he's fine! He's probably listening to an audiobook or something," Nana Rhea says, waving her off.

We each stand to give Nana Rhea a hug. She embraces me, then pulls back, her hands still tenderly holding my upper arms. "I'm sorry for snapping at you last night."

"It's okay," I say. "I understand."

She smiles. "You know, last night made me realize that maybe I do want to get back into acting. I still love that life."

"Really?"

"Yes. I guess it could be possible to still act and define my own legacy. I mean, did you see how many people were still in my fan club? And Daniel introduced me to some directors at the after-party who talked to me about a couple of interesting parts."

"Leading-lady parts?"

"Parts I think I'd like. They might want to even have me host a comedy show." She winks.

I grin.

"I'll take you to get your other ear pierced soon," Nana Rhea promises.

I don't have time to reply before she hustles out the front door. Once she's gone, Mom and Dad turn to face me.

"Do you want to go through the list of your extra summer chores now?" Dad crosses his arms.

"Can I just have one more chore-free hour?" I ask, grasping my dead phone in my hand. I need to see if Tamzin or Sadia ever texted me to invite me back. I'm not sure if it'll change anything, but I still have to know.

My parents exchange a look.

"Just one," Mom says, holding up her index finger.

"Thank you!"

I spin on my heel, hustle to my bedroom, and yank my phone charger out of my packed bag in the corner. It takes a couple seconds for the charging icon to appear on my phone screen after plugging it into the wall. I watch as my phone slowly comes to life. After what seems like a million years, notifications for tons of texts and three missed calls pop up on my screen.

Whoa.

I go through the texts and see that they are mainly from my classmates who saw me on Melly's *We Are Live!* livestream. But I swipe them away without answering them. Those can wait.

The three missed calls are all from Dad. He must've called after I left my phone in the trunk of his car. Whoops.

Then I notice a text from Tamzin. Her name on my phone screen makes my heart pound. What if this is the apology text I'd been waiting for all day yesterday?!

I quickly swipe it open to read.

we saw you on the livestream with melly and eva collins! that's soooo cool! we didn't realize you even knew who she was since you're not allowed to see her types of movies!

The next text is from Sadia in the same thread.

Yeah, that is so awesome, Audrey!

Then there is another message from Tamzin.

text us back right away when you
see these. we can't wait to hear
everything about that party.

The last text in the chat is from Sadia.

Yes OMG it looks so fun from what
we saw on the livestream.

I close out their messages and look up at the ceiling. Am I happy to get these texts? Yesterday I would've been overjoyed. But today feels... different.

When we first met, Sadia, Tamzin, and I *were* close friends. We all liked playing at the park, and we all lived pretty close to one another. However, the more I think about it, the more I realize that maybe we aren't anymore. And maybe that's okay.

I swipe open the last text message from an unknown number.

This is Eva!! Now you have my number!!!!!!!!!!!!!! ☺☺

I blink down at the message, warmth spreading through my chest. Even though I wasn't regular Audrey with Eva last night, I was more honest with her than I can ever remember being with Tamzin and Sadia. Eva actually feels like a real friend. Suddenly feeling a whole lot better, I type out a text back to Eva and hit send.

Hi Eva! Yesterday was super fun! Let's hang out again.

Her reply comes fast.

Duh! Of course we are hanging out again!!! 😁 When are you free???

I smile down at my phone.

Then pause.

Oh, right. I'm not going to be free for a long time. I'm grounded until the next century.

I think I'm going to be grounded for a bit for ditching my parents last night, but we will hang out the second I'm ungrounded!

I don't have to wait long for her response.

Tell me as soon as you're free!! And we can still text until then!

A wide grin spreads across my face. Maybe I won't be friendless next year after all.

I quickly send her a message back.

Yes we can 😁

"Audrey!" Mom calls from the living room. "Hour's up. Time to come out!"

I throw my phone on the bed, take a deep breath, and head out to the living room.

Weirdly, I catch myself still grinning as I go to accept my chores. I may be grounded all summer, and I may have to do loads of community service, but I know that no matter what next year brings, this new version of Audrey will get more chances to make choices for herself.

ACKNOWLEDGMENTS

Writing this book was my own grand adventure, and thankfully, there were many people on the exciting journey with me!

Jessica Mileo, my incredible agent. You already know how much I appreciate you, but I cannot say it enough. I'll shout it from the top of the Hollywood sign! You are a superb advocate and have taught me so much in the years we have worked together. Your guidance and support for both this book and my career are unparalleled.

My exceptional editor, Liz Kossnar. Your vision and direction for this book elevated it to a level I did not think was possible when I sat down to type out the first draft. I cherish your feedback tremendously and can't believe how lucky I am to work with you again!

Thank you to everyone at Little, Brown Books for Young Readers who helped champion this story, including Megan Tingley, Jackie Engel, Alvina Ling, Esther Reisberg, Patricia Alvarado, Maureen Klier,

Nicole Wayland, Mara Brashem, Cheryl Lew, Christie Michel, and Emilie Polster. I'm mentally sending you all enormous thank-you hugs!

Big thanks to Gabrielle Chang, who designed the fun cover, and Marta Kissi, who absolutely nailed it with the illustration!

Aisling Fowler, I'm so ridiculously fortunate to have met you. Thank you for being a wonderful middle-grade buddy.

Thank you to my wonderful writing community, including Melissa Seymour, Alyssa Colman, Graci Kim, Julie Abe, Rochelle Hassan, Alyssa Zaczek, Annabel Steadman, and so many more. Also, thanks to everyone in the #22Debuts group, especially Melissa Dassori, Ava Wilder, Erin La Rosa, Shawn Peters, Tracy Badua, and Erika Lewis.

My encouraging and supportive parents, Kymberly and Bob. Thank you for always believing in my dreams and for being the best family a girl could ask for. I love you.

Thank you to my Nana, my "educational grandma," who always champions creativity and curiosity.

And finally, thank you to my partner, Liam. You're pretty cool. Oh, also I love you.

Marta Kissi

KARINA EVANS

is the author of *Grow Up, Tahlia Wilkins!* She studied English with a concentration in film at the University of Delaware before going into a career in the entertainment industry. She currently lives in Los Angeles, California, and invites you to visit her online at karinaevans.com.